EVOLVED

N.R. WALKER

BLURB

In 2068, androids are an integrated part of human life. Big Brother no longer just watches from the shadows. It's in every household.

Lloyd Salter has OCD issues with noise and mess, and he's uncomfortable with human interaction. When his ex claimed the only thing perfect enough to live up to his standards was an android, Lloyd dismissed it. But two years later, after much self-assessment, Lloyd thinks he may have been right.

SATinc is the largest manufacturer of androids in Australia, including the Fully Compatible Units known as an A-Class 10. Their latest design is the Synthetic Human Android UNit, otherwise known as *SHAUN*.

Shaun is compatible with Lloyd's *every* need; the perfect fit on an intellectual and physical basis. But Lloyd soon realises Shaun's not like other A-Class androids. He learns. He adapts. Sure that SATinc is aware Shaun functions outside of his programmed parameters, Lloyd must find a way to keep Shaun safe.

No one can know how special Shaun is. No one can know he's evolved.

COPYRIGHT

Cover Artist: Reese Dante
Editor: Labyrinth Bound Edits
Publisher: BlueHeart Press
Evolved © 2018 N.R. Walker
First Edition 2018

EVOLVED

01100101 01110110 01101111 01101100 01110110
01100101 01100100

N.R. WALKER

CHAPTER ONE

I ARRIVED at Synthetic Android Technology Inc, or SATinc, as it was more commonly known, at ten to ten on an already cool autumn Melbourne morning. I thanked my driver, a government standard C-Class android, and got out of the vehicle.

I stood in front of the large, white, glass-wall building for a brief moment. My reflection met me. My hair matched my camel-coloured wool coat; my chocolate-brown scarf was the exact colour of my eyes, though the set of my jaw belied my nerves. I took a deep, affirming breath—today was the day I took control of my life. I fixed my coat collar, and went inside.

The interior was as sparse as the exterior. Vast shiny floors led to a seamless reception desk, the only object in the huge room. Despite twenty-foot ceilings and walls of glass, it was surprisingly warm and eerily silent. My anxiety about what environment I would be walking into eased, and I felt comfortable in the minimalistic room.

The woman behind the counter smiled at me. She was strikingly beautiful, possibly Japanese, with straight black hair and perfectly white teeth. It took me a moment to fully realise that she wasn't human. Jesus. She was so... real.

"Can I help you?" she said. Even her voice sounded real.

"Yes, my name is Lloyd Salter. I have an appointment at ten o'clock."

She didn't need to check a computer. She was one. "Yes, of course. Mr Kingsley is expecting you." She stood, walked around the side of the desk, and gestured with her hand. "This way, please."

She walked like a human, behaved like a human, spoke like a human. She was by far the most advanced synthetic android I'd seen.

She led me to a white door in the white wall, which I might not have even known existed if it hadn't opened as we approached. The hall was yet more white, though there were doors leading off the hall to what I assumed were offices. She stopped at one door in particular, which opened as if on cue, and stepped inside. "Mr Salter to see you, sir."

The man she spoke to stood at the end of his very large office, looking out through an internal window. He was younger than I'd expected. Younger than me even. He wore tailored navy suit pants and a crisp white shirt. He was rather handsome, his features even a little perfect, and I might've thought he was an android too if his smile didn't produce wrinkles at his eyes.

"Ah, Mr Salter," he greeted me as if we were old friends. He walked over to me and stood just a fraction too close. "Are you ready to change your life?"

Well, I was here, wasn't I?

"I assume for the better," I said.

His smile became a grin. "Like you can't even imagine."

Within five minutes of meeting Sasha Kingsley, I knew

several things. He was an elite salesman, and he was incredibly intelligent. Genius even. He was the mastermind behind SATinc. At thirty-four years old, he was the CEO of the biggest synthetic android company in Australia. He was astute, critical, streamlined in his conversation and movements, and I might have even liked him.

If I liked people.

And he wasted no time in getting to the point. "You've purchased the newest A-Class synthetic android," he said, slowly nodding.

I almost smiled. "I'm two hundred thousand credits shorter in my account, so I assume it's purchased."

He smiled right back at me, and I decided he was on the smarmy side of confident. A trait I didn't truly care for. He clapped his hands together, a loud noise in an otherwise silent space. "Then let's get down to business. To the showroom."

He waved his hand toward the door, much like the android receptionist had, though I was grateful he was pretty much no-nonsense after that. If he expected me to need pandering for dropping a rather large sum of money in his account, he was wrong. I didn't need my ego polished. He already had my money.

I followed him further down the hall where a set of doors opened as we approached. The room inside—the showroom, as he called it—was large and white, like everything else. But, the way a car showroom might display the best vehicles, this showroom displayed synthetic androids. And not just the full bodies, but the parts as well. Six almost naked forms, save underwear, three gynoid, three android, stood along a wall like almost naked mannequins, only very, very humanlike. There was a section of wall dedicated to hair, to eyes, to feet, to breasts, to pecs, to skin colour and texture. It was like I'd walked into a body workshop. In many ways, I guess I had.

"Something the matter?" he asked.

"I uh, I thought it would be more digital," I said. "That I'd be selecting from 3D holograms."

"Here at SATinc, we want you to know what you're getting. Especially with the A-Class, I want you to feel the hair, feel the skin." He reached out and almost touched one of the gynoids but paused. "If you were ordering ten C-Class units out of a catalogue to be fitted as tram drivers, then sure. But when customers expect the very best, they'll get exactly what they ordered."

Fair enough. I stared at the three android models. I'd researched online for quite some time, so I knew which one I preferred, but to see him up close... And nearly naked... God, the bulge in his underwear was impressive. It made me feel warm all over.

"Which model do you like?" he asked, though he didn't really need to. I hadn't stopped staring at him.

"Shaun."

"Oh, very good choice," Sasha said. "You won't be disappointed."

I walked over to the inanimate android and looked him in the eyes. My God, he was so lifelike.

"Have you owned androids before?" Sasha asked behind me.

"Yes. A driver, a cleaner."

He stood closer to me now. "But never a fully compatible unit."

I shook my head.

Fully Compatible Unit meant the android was programmed to meet my every need. Every need. Even sexual.

Especially sexual.

"You can touch him," Sasha whispered before he stepped back, giving me space. Giving me time.

I lifted my hand to Shaun and lightly touched his chest, gasping as I did.

"Feels very real, doesn't he?" Sasha sounded pleased.

I didn't turn to see his face. I nodded instead. Then I flattened my palm over Shaun's pec and slid it up to his neck. His jaw, his bottom lip. "My God."

"Shall I turn him on for you?" Sasha asked.

I nodded once. "Please."

"Shaun, Power On," Sasha said clearly, and the android in front of me blinked. Then Sasha smiled. "Like all androids, voice command operated to power up and down." He turned to the android next to Shaun. "Shane, Power On."

Shane blinked and looked at Sasha expectantly. "Shane, Power Down."

And Shane did.

Sasha walked over to stand beside me. "Shaun, this is Lloyd."

"Hello, Lloyd," Shaun said; his voice was like warmed honey. It matched his eyes. He extended his hand and I shook it.

It felt real. It felt very real, like a human hand. It was even warm.

"All modules have a running temperature of thirty-six degrees Celsius," Sasha said as if he could read my mind. "Helps enhance the human factor during intercourse."

I blanched. "Right."

Sasha put a gentle hand on my shoulder. "Let me run through some specs with you first. I'm sure you've read all about them, but it helps to establish a clinical approach.

Discussing their sexual capabilities is no different than discussing their cooking or cleaning capabilities. It's easy to empathise with them because they look human, and they're designed to look human but they're not human. I assume you read the AI Humanoid Commission Act before signing and forwarding payment?"

I nodded.

"Good. Though I'm sure you understood it perfectly well, by law I am obliged to reiterate." Then he proceeded to give me a well-rehearsed spiel, one that he'd no doubt given a thousand times before. "The International Roboethics Act and the AI Humanoid Rights Commission Act is a law under Australian Federal legislation that sets industry standards and the legal rights of all androids. There are certain laws that are obvious, such as the prohibition of child androids, but also the intricate laws that deal with ethics and consent. There are common laws that ensure no malice or deliberate harm comes to any android, and with the introduction of All Purpose Units, laws pertaining to consent.

"All sexual relations must be consensual, which companies such as SATinc have ensured by programming sexual desire into their synthetic androids. Yes, sexual desire. Not programmed to say 'yes' if asked, but actual desire. Neural networks within their mainframe recognise their owner's face, body, and their synthetic hormone sensors react accordingly, all within the Roboethics Guidelines of course. By law, all of SATinc's units also have built-in security features, which enable an automatic shutdown and the AMA, the Artificial Moral Agency, and the police are notified should the unit's pain receptors be activated. In accordance with our mission statement, SATinc prides itself on integrity and all customers are subject to full background checks, yourself included."

I resisted giving him applause for his performance. "I trust you found no red flags."

He humoured me with a smile. "Of course. I trust you're happy with the contractual terms and conditions within these laws."

I signed the contract, didn't I? "Of course."

"Excellent. Though I'm happy to address any concerns you might have."

"I have no concerns."

"Good. But our products are also a purpose-built unit. They are purchased for a purpose; a range of reasons, really, including sexual activity. They are designed for it. So, we can get all those details out of the way before we choose aesthetics, yes?"

I nodded. "Yes."

"All units are temperature controlled, waterproof, and self-cleaning. You can help him clean himself, but he is capable of doing so on his own." Then he turned to Shaun. "Shaun, please take off your underwear."

I could have sworn the android smirked. But then he slid his fingers under the elastic of his briefs and slid them down to the floor. He picked them up, folded them, and set them on the desk.

Oh boy.

"Very life-like, yes?"

His cock hung heavy, great girth and length. It was unnerving, in a totally arousing kind of way. I nodded. "Yes."

"Would you like to touch it?"

I spun to look at Sasha. "No. That would be... inappropriate."

Sasha gave me a tight smile. "He's here for display purposes, Mr Salter. If you were buying a new car, would it be inappropriate to touch it?"

"Well, no."

"This is no different." He paused, and I was certain he wanted to sigh but didn't.

I said, "Laws state you can't touch an android without consent."

"Under Section Five of the Rights Act, it states all display units can be handled accordingly, for the purposes of selection and sale."

I studied Shaun. "It's just that he looks so real."

Sasha chuckled. "Thank you." Then he said, "Shaun, please take your penis in your hand."

Shaun did.

"He has the seven and a half inch," Sasha said casually. "And I'm sure you read all about genital development before you decided to buy."

I felt myself blush. "Yes, I did."

He spoke like I hadn't answered. "It's been quite the advancement in PSE, the silicone we use for his skin, but the A-Class 10, which is the model you've purchased, has penile capabilities of lengthening and pulsing at point of climax."

I let out a slow breath. "I read that, yes." I'd watched many videos on the penile capabilities, which was probably why I couldn't stop watching Shaun holding his cock. He was only holding it; he hadn't been instructed to stroke. Thankfully.

"Would you like to see it in action?"

Oh boy. I cleared my throat. "Ah, that won't be necessary," I said. I sat down at the desk and pretended an anatomically perfect, naked android wasn't standing two metres away with his perfect cock in his hand.

Sasha sat opposite me and activated some hologram screens. "Okay, so we have your psychological report already. We use these findings to program the unit so you're compatible on a psychological level: which social intelligence, automated reasoning parameters are best suited to you. But we'll start with some information about you to help me understand you and best program your unit."

It was almost a relief that he already knew I had OCD tendencies and misophonia, and I didn't have to say it out loud. I let out a steady breath. "Yes, please."

"Age?"

"Forty-one."

"Your profession?"

"Professor of Philosophy at Melbourne University."

"Interesting," he mused.

"Well, if you're wondering about my stance on phenomenology and existentialism and what that means in the world of androids, I think we'll need a longer appointment."

He studied me for a second, then smirked, and basically ignored me. "Hobbies?"

I cleared my throat. "Reading. I have an extensive library on historical literature, and I'd love for my android to be well versed in this also."

Sasha nodded. "Done. Any other hobbies?"

"Movies, I guess." I shifted in my seat. "I prefer to stay at home."

Sasha continued as if I wasn't some introverted, socially inept man. He looked up from his screen and smiled. "It suits our units better to be homebodies. Given they need full wireless interconnectivity to your home hub router."

I knew this. "Yes, that's probably for the best."

"You can take your unit out and away from your Wi-Fi for a period of no longer than fourteen days. If you plan on travelling for longer periods than that, you just need to let us know. We can ensure your unit connects to a router wherever you're staying. It's no problem. So if you want to take him on a weekend trip or a week in the mountains or to a two-week work conference, or around the world for a year, you have that freedom."

"Okay." It wasn't likely. I rarely left Melbourne for any longer than a day. "That's good to know."

"In the information you submitted with your application, you were asked what you found attractive in a mate. You answered intelligence, conversation, confidence."

"Yes, that's correct."

"You also specified the unit must adhere to certain preferences. You can't tolerate the sound of people chewing, loud breathing, snoring."

My heart squeezed at the casual mention of my misophonia triggers. I swallowed. "Yes, that's correct."

"Then your unit will be perfect for you. No mess, no noise, and will always adhere to your house cleanliness standards."

I breathed out slowly. "Good."

"What about physical attributes?"

I glanced quickly at Shaun, who was still standing beside me, penis in hand. "Um."

Sasha could read people well enough to know I wasn't comfortable.

"I'm not a prude, exactly," I explained. Which wasn't exactly true. "It's just I find him rather distracting."

Sasha turned to the android. "Shaun, please put your underpants back on."

Shaun did.

God. The bulge in the underwear was more of a turn-on.

When I looked back at Sasha, he was smiling at me. "You ready to build your dream man?"

I ignored the tightening in my belly. "Yes."

I left an hour later, too embarrassed to be nervous. Choosing hair and eye colour, height, and voice tenor was all easy compared to discussing what kind of ribbing I wanted in the throat and anal cavity.

But it was done. I was now the legal custodian of a Class-A *SHAUN*. Synthetic Human Android UNit. I just had to wait three months while he was handcrafted, calibrated, and then my fully compatible synthetic android would be delivered.

Three months, and then I wouldn't be alone anymore.

CHAPTER TWO

THREE MONTHS LATER

I WALKED into the staff break room just in time to hear Mrs Van Der Heek say, "I just don't think it's right. I get that androids are a part of everyday life. I have no problem with that. They do all the menial tasks that humans don't, so I can appreciate their usefulness, but those synthetic androids...," she said like the words tasted bad. She gave a visible shudder. "It's not right."

I froze. Did she know? How did she find out? No, there was no way she could know. *Nobody knows...*

"Professor Salter," she said. "How do you feel about those Class-A synthetic dirtybots?"

Dirtybots. The word unleashed a bubble of anger through me but I hid it well. "I don't think it's anyone's place to judge," I said coolly. "If you don't like them, don't get one."

She blinked, and a few other professors smirked. Old Mrs Van Der Heek was a dinosaur, in age and ethics. It was a shame her mouth wasn't as closed as her worldviews.

"Well, I believe it goes against God," she went on to say.

And her bigotry was Jurassic as well.

I placed my salad neatly in front of me and straightened my fork so it was perfectly in line, adjacent and parallel to all other lines. A lifelong habit. An OCD habit.

I ignored Mrs Van Der Heek as she soon started talking about the good old days before robotics. It was something she ranted about often, an argument we'd all heard from her before. The fact that she used Class-C and Class-B androids for driving and cleaning made her a hypocrite.

The world was, unfortunately, full of hypocrites.

"So, you've got some extra leave?" Jae asked me. Jae Jin was the faculty IT guy, and despite me not knowing him overly well, he was probably my only true friend at the university. We had a lot in common. He ate silently, breathed soundlessly, and always arranged his lunch in perfect order. He was neatly dressed at all times, though he had a penchant for wearing shades of brown. His thick jet-black framed glasses matched his hair, and he had traces of OCD, though I never asked him outright. We were just drawn to each other's company.

Birds of a feather and all that.

"Yes, a week," I explained.

"Travelling away?"

"No, family time," I lied. It wasn't that I was close to my family at all—I wasn't—but this was personal time. I could hardly explain to him that I was taking the time to become acquainted with my synthetic android. I didn't want Shaun to arrive and for me to leave him at home by himself. I'm sure many people did, but it didn't feel right to me.

Jae grimaced sympathetically. He came from a large Korean family and his parents lived with him, and although he was true to his culture, I knew some days he appreciated solitude. "Maybe just a short day trip then," he said. "The Great Ocean Drive is pretty this time of year."

I chewed my mouthful of salad thoughtfully. Could I be so brazen as to take Shaun for a drive? It did seem a rather romantic notion and I wondered if Shaun would like it. I wondered about a lot of things Shaun might like. "That's a good idea," I allowed.

"Well, enjoy your time off." He went on to sigh quietly and proclaim his thankfulness that mid-terms were over for another year. Classes weren't due to wrap up for another few weeks yet, and I would no doubt spend the actual week-long break getting ready for the next semester so this week was solely for Shaun. It was recommended that all new custodians of A-Class Synths take time to help integrate their android. A whole week was probably ambitious, but my anticipation thought it best. It also gave me time to get used to sharing my space with another being.

Jae shot old Mrs Van Der Heek a hardened glare. "Does she ever know when to shut up?" he whispered to me.

I'd been too caught up thinking about Shaun and hadn't heard what she'd said, but I liked that Jae and I were of the same opinion about her. I smiled. "Apparently not. Is she still going on about synthetics and God?"

He rolled his eyes and fixed his glasses. "If an android were allowed to replace her, I'd fund it myself."

I chuckled, and for a brief moment, I considered telling him about my delivery tomorrow. But fear and privacy stopped me, and the fact it was an android and not a gynoid. I'd out myself in more ways than one. "You and me both. We could halve the cost."

Jae smiled and neatly folded his lunch wrapper and set it on the table at a perfect ninety degrees from the edge. Yes, I liked him a lot.

"Well, have fun on your break," he said.

Nervous butterflies swarmed my belly. "I'm sure I will, thank you."

───────────

BY THE TIME my intercom sounded at nine fifteen the next morning, the butterflies in my belly felt more like stomping elephants. I buzzed the delivery team through and waited for the elevator to *ping* down the hall.

Breathe, Lloyd, I reminded myself.

My apartment was a spacious two-bedroom luxury unit on the top floor of the complex. Polished concrete floors, high ceilings, a bookcase as one entire wall, and floor-to-ceiling windows on the north-east facing wall. I liked the clean lines, minimalistic furniture. Well, I didn't just like it. I needed it. Clutter and closed spaces made me anxious. My ex-boyfriend had found my apartment cold and clinical, but I found the whites and greys soothing, peaceful. Then again, he'd found a lot of things about me clinical...

The knock on my door startled me, even though I'd been expecting it. I opened it to find two men and a rather large crate. The first man smiled. He was wearing grey suit pants and a navy sweater. He showed me his ID. "Mr Salter, my name is Myles Dewegger. We have a special delivery."

"Yes, yes, please come in," I said, standing aside in invitation.

The second man wheeled through the crate. He was dressed all in black with a military style haircut, and he looked as though he belonged in a SWAT team. He was a rather large man, with bulging muscles and perfect skin, and I had to study him for a second. No, he was human.

"Nice place," Myles said, looking around the large, open living room. "Are we all right to do this here?"

I closed the door and took a breath to steady myself. I wasn't accustomed to having strange people in my house. "Yes, of course." I followed him and stood next to the couch. "I thought Mr Kingsley might have attended the delivery. I assumed incorrectly, it seems."

"Sasha's a busy man," Myles said with a smile. "Though if you'd prefer, I can call him and you can speak to him."

"No, it's fine," I said. I was now staring at the crate. *Oh boy*. It was well over six feet tall, three feet wide. Shaun was inside. He was right there. I swallowed hard.

Myles read me. "Let's introduce you, shall we?"

I nodded. "Yes, please."

Myles and his helper, whose name I didn't know, undid the crate and removed the front panel. My heart almost stopped. Inside, Shaun stood, packaged-in perfectly so as not to be damaged in any way. He was dressed in a dinner suit. A charming navy piece with a light blue shirt underneath his blazer, top button undone. His black hair was exactly as I'd ordered; short sides, longer on top, professional. His skin was warm ivory with a subtle hint of blush on his cheeks; his lips were pink and a perfect cupid's bow. His eyes were closed, his lashes long.

He took my breath away.

The big delivery guy stepped in and unstrapped Shaun, then lifted him out. Right, that explained the need for muscle. Then he quickly wheeled the crate back to the front door, making the room neat again, leaving Shaun standing perfectly still in my living room.

Myles glanced at me. "Everything look okay?"

I nodded and had to focus on speaking so I could make actual sound. "So far, yes."

Myles smiled. "So first we need to configure him to your home hub," he said, looking around.

I pointed to the small black unit on the cabinet behind the dining table. It was a small, black disc, much like an ice hockey puck. It was my central router and connected all aspects of my life to the internet. Every home had one. Connectivity was integral to living in the mid-twenty-first century. It connected everything from grocery orders to financial accounts, home security to social security details. Big Brother no longer just watched. Big Brother was in every aspect of our lives. Each home hub was voice activated and accessible only to nominated residents in each house.

"Home hub On," I said, and the hologram panel appeared.

Myles took out a small hand-held screen I recognised from the SATinc office. It was a control panel. He tapped on both screens, I entered in a personal code, and Shaun was officially added to my Wi-Fi.

It was becoming so very real.

Myles seemed completely unfazed and oblivious to the fact that I was in the middle of a monumental life event. He went on a spiel of specifications and diagnostics, developmental robotics, neural networks, artificial consciousness, proprioceptive sensors, and spatial cognizance, but all I could do was stare at Shaun.

Breathe, Lloyd.

Myles stopped speaking when he realised I wasn't paying attention, and his pause made me look at him instead. He continued, "I'll activate him, then we'll require him to study your face for a few seconds. He has facial recognition, so once he recognises you as his custodian, he'll be able to identify you anywhere."

"Okay."

"So if you're out in public and you become separated, he will be able to find you."

For the strangest reason, I found that comforting.

"And your voice. He'll recognise that anywhere."

I smiled at Shaun, though he still had his eyes closed.

"Are you ready?" Myles asked.

I nodded.

Myles held the small black screen toward me. He entered in a code and spoke clear and loud. "Please re-enter in your Wi-Fi code," he said, averting his eyes while I entered my security code for Shaun's wireless access. Then Myles added something else, and watching Shaun, he said, "Activate."

Shaun opened his eyes.

They were the exact shade of blue I'd asked for. But he just stared blankly.

Myles entered in more codes, then spoke to me. "Please stand in front of him until I tell you to move."

I did as I was instructed. Shaun was approximately an inch shorter than me, and he was even better close up. Being this close to him sent a curl of anticipation through me.

I could hear Myles tapping on the screen and then Shaun's eyes focused on me. He was scanning my face, and then he looked down to my feet and up my body. It set my blood on fire.

Then Myles handed me the small screen and said, "Please read this out loud to him."

I let out a breath and looked Shaun right in the eye. "My name is Lloyd Salter. I am your custodian, and this is your home."

Myles took the control again and clicked on the screen a

few more times, and something in Shaun changed. I saw it, the very moment it happened.

He became aware.

His gaze fell on me. "Hello, Lloyd," Shaun said. His voice was a deep baritone, with a tenor that curled in my belly.

"Hello Shaun," I replied. My voice was barely a whisper.

And then, throwing my world completely off its axis, he smiled. Not a perfect smile, but slightly lopsided in a very human way. If a simple smile could complete my existence, it was done. He was stunningly perfect.

"It is very nice to meet you," Shaun said.

"Likewise," I replied. I couldn't stop staring at his eyes, and I swore the corner of Shaun's lip twitched in an almost smile.

"Is that normal?" I asked Myles. "He's so... human."

Myles grinned. "It's amazing, isn't it? How real they are?"

I nodded, staring back at Shaun. So very real.

"As I was saying before, he has the spatial awareness and object manipulation skills of a surgeon. He can lift heavy objects with ease, but he can also hold the finest, most delicate glass object with precision. He has social intelligence; he can recognise and interpret, process and simulate human affects and empathy. He is, without doubt, the most advanced A-Class synthetic android in the world."

Shaun tilted his head a little while he studied me, and I stared right back at him. *So remarkable.*

"He's been uploaded with extensive knowledge of all requested data," Myles said, holding the screen out for me to see. I glanced at it but couldn't take my eyes off Shaun for long. Myles continued anyway. "Literary histories, world current affairs, everything you asked for has been preloaded, but he can access any information you require. If it's on the web, he can find it, and he can discuss, converse, debate whatever you want."

Wow.

"Now, as for the personal companion aspect," Myles went on. Personal companion aspect was synthetic speak for sex. "All lubricants must be silicone based, not oil based, though I'm sure you're aware. He can self-clean but he might like it if you help him." I looked at Myles and he winked. "Yes, he has likes and dislikes. Though he's been pre-dispositioned to your psych evaluation so there are no conflicts. He enjoys conversation, attention, praise..., touch. Sex."

My heart rate took off.

Breathe, Lloyd.

Shaun looked at me and his lip started to pull up on one side. I already knew that smirk would be devastating. I had to tell myself to swallow, and I pretended the curl of heat in my belly wasn't desire.

"He likes sex?" I knew this already, but my brain was stuck on that damn smirk.

"Oh, yes." Myles tapped away on the control panel. "Though I am legally obliged to tell you that if he's subject to things he doesn't like, like abuse, torture, non-consensual sex, sex with someone that is not you, regardless if he is powered on or off, he's programmed to alert the AMA."

I knew this also. The AMA, or Artificial Moral Agency, was the governing body of Roboethics. Androids of all classes were granted rights under the Geneva Convention, and if any harm were to come to an android, they were all programmed to alert the officials. "Yes, of course. I fully support the law."

Myles looked up briefly, afforded me a smile that said *of course you do*. Then he gave me the rundown on Shaun's ability to do housework and some cooking ability, though thermoplastic elastomer—what Shaun's skin was made out of—didn't react too well to extreme heat.

I knew that too.

Myles continued to give me a crash course in operation, explaining the full manual was in the control panel, but Shaun was now programmed to respond to my voice alone.

"Shaun, Power Down," Myles said.

Shaun looked at him but didn't power down. "You are not authorised," Shaun replied.

Myles gave me a nod. "Your turn."

I looked at Shaun. "Shaun, Power Down."

Shaun's hands went to his sides, his eyes closed, and his head bowed slightly.

Something inside me lurched, saddened even. It felt wrong to decide when he was and wasn't awake, but before I could tell him to power up, Myles handed me the control panel.

"Sign here to say you've received your unit."

I quickly read the screen and signed.

He signed underneath my signature and handed the control panel back to me. "Congratulations. You're now the legal custodian of Shaun. If you have any questions, issues, or need anything at all, contact us at any time."

"Uh, yes. Thank you. I will."

He and the big muscled guy collected the crate, let themselves out, and I was left alone with my new Synthetic Human Android UNit.

Shaun.

I studied him for a second. He was completely still, powered down, and he looked peaceful. I reached out and almost touched his cheek, but it felt wrong to do so without his consent.

I took a step back, took a deep breath, and let it out slowly. "Shaun, Power Up."

He opened his eyes and lifted his head. When his gaze met mine, he smiled. "Hello, Lloyd."

"Hello, Shaun." I wasn't sure what to say next. I looked around the room.

"Are you nervous?" Shaun asked. "Your heart rate is elevated and your pupils are dilated."

"You can see that?"

"Of course. I am designed to be attuned to you."

Oh boy. Breathe Lloyd. "Uh, yes. I'm a little nervous. I've been waiting for you for a while, and I'm very happy you're here."

Shaun smiled. "I am happy to be here."

He was happy? Was he really happy, as in emotionally uplifted, or was it just a phrase?

I realised then I was still holding the control panel. I walked over to the cabinet and slid it on top. When I turned around, Shaun had turned and was watching me. "Would you like me to show you your new home?"

"Yes, please."

"This is the main living area," I said. Waving my hand at the sofas and the dining table. "Kitchen is through there." The truth was, the kitchen was sleek and state of the art with views overlooking the Yarra River and Southbank, Melbourne, but would he appreciate that? I didn't think so. "This way is the private quarters." I slid back a recessed door to reveal a hall. I didn't often close the door, but given I was expecting the delivery people, I didn't want them seeing my personal space. Not that I had anything to hide. I just liked my privacy. I needed it. It was my sanctuary, my peace of mind from the chaos, mess, and noise of the outside world. I opened the first door. "This is your room."

He moved fluidly, humanly. *God, he looked so real.* "Will I not be staying in your room with you?"

I blinked. "Oh, um. Well, uh... I just thought you might like your own space."

"If you do not wish me to join you in your room, you only have to say."

I studied him for a second. God, did he look sad or was that just my imagination?

I opened the door to the walk-in robe. "I bought you some clothes," I said. "I thought you might like to choose what you wear each day."

He looked at the clothes hanging, neat rows of sweaters, shirts, and pants. "You bought these for me?"

I hadn't anticipated he would stand so close to me so he could see inside the closet. It made my heart rate take off. "Yes."

He shot me a look. "Your heart rate is elevated." Then he straightened, but he didn't move back an inch. His voice was deep but quiet, soothing even. "You like me being close to you."

Oh boy. I stepped away and ignored his statement. If he was going to voice my every reaction... "There's an en suite bathroom also," I said, opening the other door. "You can use anything in this house at any time. You don't need to ask."

Then I walked back to the hall and showed him the main bathroom. "This is the bathroom guests use," I explained.

"Do we have guests often?"

We. He said we.

My heart galloped again, but he thankfully didn't comment. I could only assume he picked up on my earlier discomfort. God, it was bad enough I was awkward with humans, but now I was awkward with androids as well.

"Uh, no. I haven't had many guests in the past, and not for some time. I like my privacy, and I like things... a certain way." That was probably putting my OCD mildly. "I prefer things in order and I enjoy quiet."

I'd said that line a hundred times in my life. To work associates, friends, therapists, and my ex-boyfriend, and they all judged or responded as if I was broken and they could offer advice to fix me. But Shaun smiled at me. "I like those things too."

My heart raced again, but this time it was from relief, gratitude, fondness even. His quiet, peaceful demeanour was so utterly perfect for me. I blinked a few times to clear my thoughts and showed him to my bedroom. I opened the door and almost reluctantly stepped inside. "This is my room."

He walked in, taking in his surroundings. My room was quite large, with polished concrete floors, white walls, and white bedding, and charcoal grey artworks above the bed. Shaun did a slow 360, then stopped when he was facing me.

"Do you like it?" I asked, perplexed by his reaction. Did the white and grey bother one of his sensors? Or did he think it was cold and detached.

"It's very peaceful," he said.

It felt like the air was sucked out of the room, and I struggled to catch my breath, in a head-rush, remarkable kind of way. No one had understood that. Certainly not Ian. My ex had hated this room. I'd always said it made me calm, but he said he felt like he was in a museum, and that was not a compliment. But Shaun got it. Programmed to like what I liked or not, the relief I felt was unprecedented.

"Thank you," I whispered.

Shaun studied me for a moment, tilting his head just so. Then, in two very humanlike steps, he stood in front of me. "Do you wish to have sex with me?" he asked.

I blinked in shock and dry swallowed. It took me a few attempts at speaking, but I finally managed to get my answer out.

"No."

CHAPTER THREE

SHAUN WENT DEATHLY STILL. Still, even for an android. "Pardon me," he said gently, retreating a step. God, was he sad? "I misread your physical reaction."

"No, you didn't," I said quickly. He tilted his head and I closed my eyes and shook my head. "I'm confusing you, sorry."

He stood still, waiting for instruction or for me to explain. Just waiting.

"Shaun, we need to talk." It didn't feel right standing in my bedroom having this conversation. "Let's go to the living room."

I led the way and he followed. He really did move very lifelike. It was so remarkable, and I knew some people were freaked out by just how real the new Class-A androids were, but not me. I loved it.

I pulled a chair out at the dining table. "Please, take a seat."

He sat, and it was only then that his android form was obvious. He sat too straight to be human. He was completely posture perfect; feet together, hands resting on his knees, back straight.

I sat in the chair next to him but turned toward him, our knees almost touching. I had one hand on the table, one on my thigh. This was my space, and I was comfortable here. He was my android, so not only was I his custodian, I was also responsible for his learning and adaptation into my world. This wasn't going to be an easy conversation for me, but it was one we needed to have.

"You didn't misread anything," I said as calmly as I could, ignoring how my heart was trying to claw its way out my throat. "I am physically attracted to you."

That was true, I couldn't deny it. Being technosexual wasn't something I'd ever considered until my last argument with Ian when he'd told me if I wanted someone who was silent and tidy, so utterly perfect, I should date a robot. Two years on, and there was more truth to his words than I'd realised. It wasn't perfection I was attracted to, it was structure and order. It was everything being in perfect order that I needed, an attribute of my OCD that Ian couldn't live up to.

That no human could live up to.

But an android could.

"You were designed to be a complete fit to my life. Physically, you're very..." I let out an unsteady breath and heat spread across my cheeks. "You're very handsome."

Shaun tilted his head and slowly lifted his hand to lightly touch my face. "Your capillaries have expanded to allow increased blood flow, causing a rush of colour to temporarily stain your cheeks."

I chuckled. "Yes."

"I like it."

Just as well because I blushed even harder.

He did that head-tilt thing that I found utterly adorable. "May I ask you questions?"

"Yes, of course. You can ask me anything."

"If I am physically appealing to you, why do you not wish to enjoy sexual intercourse with me?"

Oh boy. "You're very forthright," I allowed, giving myself some time to answer.

"Is that wrong?"

"No. Not at all. In fact, I prefer it over dishonesty, and I don't want you to censor yourself." I studied him for a second, his inquisitive eyes, his perfect nose, his kissable lips... "And while I would like to eventually enjoy being physical with you, I think we should date first."

"Date," he repeated. "A social or romantic appointment or engagement."

"Yes." His dictionary definition was accurate. "So we can get to know each other first. If I met a man, a human man, and was attracted to him, I would want to know him better before I went to bed with him. I don't think you should be any different."

He blinked like it was a foreign concept. I guessed as a personal companion, sex was assumed. No doubt Myles and the delivery guy assumed I'd already be balls deep inside him before they reached the elevator, but that's not who I was.

"If we're dating, we would do things like hold hands and get to know one another."

Shaun smiled. "Would you like to hold my hand?"

I swallowed hard and smiled back at him. "Yes, I would."

He held out his hand between us, palm up. I slowly moved my hand to his and let my fingertips trace over his palm.

He felt so real.

Warm, textured, perfect.

His smile widened and his gaze shot from his hand to my eyes. "That feels nice."

I almost laughed. "It does." Then I ghosted my palm across his, letting him enjoy the new sensations. "This is all new to you," I said. It wasn't a question.

He nodded, still marvelling over our hands. And that was the reason right there that I wanted to take my time with him. I would never take a human virgin and simply bend him over my bed and bury myself in him without regard for his well-being. Why would I do that with Shaun?

Regardless of the fact he wasn't human, he was still seeing the world for the first time, and I wanted him to learn the beauty of the small things.

I threaded our fingers and he grinned. "You like that?" I asked.

His answer was serene. "Yes."

"I'm certain we will evolve to a more physical relationship," I explained. "But the anticipation is just as enjoyable."

"Anticipation," he said, his eyes intensifying. "A feeling of excitement about something that is going to happen in the near future."

I nodded. "Yes." And if he kept looking at me like that, it would be the very near future.

I needed a distraction, and my stomach reminded me right then that I'd forgone breakfast in my nervousness about Shaun's arrival. "I'm going to get myself some lunch. Would you like to join me in the kitchen?"

He nodded once. "I would like that very much."

I stood up, our hands still joined. He rose fluidly, still smiling. I fixed our hands so it was more of a palm hold, and gently pulled him toward the kitchen, but whereas a human might realise I'd need two hands to get myself some food, he never let go of my hand.

"Um," I said, smiling at him. "I'll need my hand back."

"Oh." He let go, startled. "Apologies."

I gently touched his arm. "It's perfectly fine." I opened the fridge and looked at the rows of neatly stacked prepared meals. Some people still chose to make their own, though the mess of cooking, or even sandwich making, bothered me. All I had to do was take out which ever I felt like, open, and eat. Today's lunch would be a whole wheat salad sandwich. I took it from the fridge, carefully unwrapped it, set it perfectly on my plate, and discarded the wrapper. When I was done, I took my plate and bottled water. "Will you sit at the table with me?"

He sat in his seat, straight-backed, and smiled. It was a little awkward that he would sit there and watch me eat in silence, so I needed to prompt conversation. I swallowed my first mouthful. "I work at the university, and I teach philosophy."

"Which are your favourite subjects?"

"I find the issues of applied ethics interesting, but I love the history of philosophy. Ancient Eastern, Greek, Later Antiquity."

Shaun nodded and glanced at my wall of books. "And you enjoy reading ancient books."

I smiled. "They're not exactly ancient. Paper books aren't popular, but I do prefer them. But yes, I love reading. All forms of literature, from all periods."

"You prefer this subject of literature over your chosen profession," he stated simply. "Your pupils dilate and your verbal cues are more animated."

I couldn't help but chuckle, despite the heat I could feel spread across my cheeks.

He studied me further. "And the capillaries in your cheeks expand to increase blood flow resulting in a slight reddish hue of your face. This depicts blush."

I took in a deep breath and steeled myself. "Yes, it does." I distracted myself with another bite of my sandwich and swallowed it while he watched. "And yes, I do prefer the history of literature over philosophy. Philosophy is my job, and I do love it. But literature is my passion."

"Are the two not intertwined?" He tilted his head in a curious fashion. "Historical literature and philosophy?"

I stared at him. No one had ever been so interested in this before. "Yes," I whispered. "Quite often."

"And in the history of literature, which is your favourite period?"

"The beginning, until now."

One corner of Shaun's lips curled in that heart-stopping smirk. "Early Egyptian hieroglyphics or ancient Chinese findings are most extraordinary."

I put my sandwich down, wondering if this was a test or not. I also wondered which information had been downloaded into his CPU; I'd specifically asked to be able to discuss topics of books with him. But for him to choose Egyptian and Chinese literature definitely felt like a test. "There are many who believe hieroglyphics and Chinese scribes are not literature," I added, testing the waters.

"It might be true that writings and literature, although connected, are not synonymous," Shaun replied. "And not everything written at that time might be literature as it is known today. Though, can it not be argued that hieroglyphics was literature of its time?"

I fought a smile. I liked this. I liked it a lot. "Possibly."

"Are hieroglyphs not poetic? Or can literature only be classified as such when it is written on paper?"

"*That* is still an argument amongst scholars. After thousands of years, there will always be differing opinions."

"And your opinion?"

"I believe, given the very definition of literature, that if it was written in any form and found to be of cultural value, then it is literature."

Shaun gave a nod. "And what does the Academia insist you teach?"

I grinned at him. "I teach my students to think for themselves and draw their own conclusions."

"That's very reasonable of you."

I smiled as I chewed the last of my sandwich. "Do you have an opinion?"

His eyes gleamed, and I remembered Myles saying Shaun would like conversation. "I have automated reasoning and the ability to process data, recognising favourable or unfavourable decisions."

"The ability to distinguish between right or wrong?"

"Yes. If I process historical data, I can determine if human interaction was wrong or right. I have a moral and ethical scale from which I can formulate reasonable conclusions, based on all information available."

I nodded slowly. That was more than most humans I knew. "I like that. So, back to my original question. Do you have an opinion on what constitutes historical literature?"

Shaun smiled. "Yes, I do. Where you believe any writing of cultural significance is literature, I form the opinion that literature, in its broadest sense, is any single body of written works. Much like you, I believe date and origin are not deciding factors, be it ancient Chinese or Egyptian. And if it predates religious affirmation, that does not discredit it as a source of literature. Just because one scholar chooses to believe his findings superior over a fellow scholar because of religious or spiritual beliefs, does not change the fact that it is literature."

And so it began.

A lengthy, in-depth conversation about histories of the written word and human civilisations in antiquity leading up to the modern period. His knowledge was vast and incredibly accurate; his ability to recall dates and references was astounding.

We talked well into late evening, and it wasn't until my stomach growled that he stopped mid-conversation about Jane Austen. "Are you hungry?"

"A little," I allowed. "I hadn't realised the time."

"Oh, should I remind you at certain intervals?"

"No. There's no need." I gave him a smile. "I have a feeling our conversations will be long and often. I'll get used to it."

"Are you not used to discussing subjects at such length?"

I almost laughed. "Hardly. I could talk about it for days, though not many humans share my enthusiasm."

He blinked. "Should I have not—"

I put my hand on his arm to stop him. "I have enjoyed today, very much." The truth was, I couldn't remember having such a good time.

He stared at me for a long moment before he smiled. "I have enjoyed today very much also."

I stood up. "Will you join me in the kitchen? I need to make myself some dinner."

He stood and followed me. "Would you rather I retrieved you a sandwich? I studied your efforts when you prepared one earlier and I can now replicate."

I smiled at him again. "Another time maybe. I was going to get myself something different for dinner. You're welcome to watch."

"Thank you."

I took another prepared meal from the fridge and placed it into the heat replicating oven. He stood to the side and observed, and I couldn't help but smile at him. He was learning by watching. I was sure I could tell him to search his neural networks for recipes and he could reproduce them with precision, and he could very well clean up after himself, but it was nice to do this with him. It was a human thing to do. And when I reached across the counter for my silicone mitt, he handed it to me.

I was stunned, quite frankly. He anticipated my move?

"Pre-emptive recognition," he explained.

I took the mitt, our fingers brushed, and a bloom of warmth settled in my belly. "Thank you."

He smiled. "You are welcome."

THAT EVENING, after I'd eaten, I took the controller and sat on the sofa with it. "I have so much to learn about you," I said.

Shaun sat beside me, so close I could feel his thermal heat. "Or you could ask me?"

Looking at him, at his clear blue eyes and perfect face, the rush of anticipation returned. God, I could tell him right now that we should test his sexual components, and he would. And I wanted to. The warmth in my belly spread lower to my groin at the thought...

But no, it wouldn't be right.

"Okay," I started, gathering my thoughts. "To recharge, do you need to power down?"

"No, I do not require to power down to recharge. For as long as I am within your home Wi-Fi range, I remain fully charged. And with my lithium A-Class battery cells, I can run indefinitely."

"Okay good." I didn't like telling him to power down, so that suited me just fine. "So tonight, when I sleep, what will you do?"

"I will ensure you are comfortable at all times. Do you like having company in your bed while you sleep?"

"Oh, I... Uh, I..."

"It was not my intention to make you nervous."

"I'm not," I lied. Then I realised I had no reason to lie to him. In fact, if he was going to be compatible to my every need, I shouldn't lie to him. "Okay, I'm nervous." And that was the whole truth. "I do like having someone in my bed. Although it's been a long time..."

Shaun gave a nod. "Then I shall stay beside you and ensure you are comfortable." He smiled a little. "And I can ensure such things like your coffee is ready the moment you wake."

God. According to him, going to bed with me and making my coffee were on equal standing.

He tilted his head and he spoke quietly. "Lloyd, may I ask something of you?"

Oh boy. The way he said my name... "Yes."

"May I hold your hand? People hold hands when they date," he furthered. "And if we are dating, then we would hold hands, yes?"

"Yes." I smiled and offered him my hand, palm up. He took it carefully in his own and smiled right back at me. "You like it?" I asked.

"Yes. I have exteroceptive sensors on certain parts of my

body that record tactile responses which can be likened to human endorphins. I like it very much."

I tried very hard not to think about where those other certain parts of his body were. "Well, I'm glad. I like it too."

"And I trust you will inform me when you wish to further our dating courtship."

I fought a smile at first, but his seriousness and imploring eyes and his close proximity sobered me. "I will. I'll take it slow and you can tell me what you do and don't like."

His smile became serene and he gently squeezed my hand. "Well, I like this very much."

I liked it very much too. I liked *him* very much. Already. I liked that he was so immaculately presented and postured. There was no mess, no noise, no human faults.

"Well, it's getting late," I said. "I might get ready for bed. I like to read before I sleep."

Shaun nodded. "Very well." He stood first this time and, still holding my hand, gently helped me to my feet.

But after I came out of the bathroom dressed for bed, he was still wearing his blazer and suit pants. Not that he would be uncomfortable if he lay down in them, but it wouldn't feel right to me. "Here," I said, helping him out of his jacket. "Let me take this for you. I'll hang it in your wardrobe and get some pyjamas for you so you can get changed."

I hung his blazer in his wardrobe and grabbed some sleeping boxers and an undershirt, not really thinking about what I'd said to him, how he'd interpret that as a literal instruction. But when I walked back into my room, he stood there wearing only a pair of briefs. His body was perfectly sculptured, the physique of a swimmer. He was everything I'd asked for when I designed him. He was literally my dream man, everything I wanted. And the bulge in his briefs... his balls looked tight and heavy, his cock lay snug toward his hip, permanently half-hard—only fully hardening when his sensors were aroused.

I licked my lips and my own cock stirred.

"You like what you see," he said.

"Very much."

"You can touch me," Shaun said. "Anywhere you want."

Warmth flooded my veins and my cock filled, begging for attention.

Shaun looked from my crotch to my eyes. "Do you want to touch me?"

I couldn't breathe. I couldn't speak. I wanted to touch him, every part of him. I wanted to bury myself inside him and lose myself forever.

Shaun smirked and slid his fingers underneath his briefs to remove them, and I tried to form some kind of reply.

Oh boy.

CHAPTER FOUR

"LEAVE THEM ON," I said. My voice held no conviction but he complied. I handed him the sleep shorts and T-shirt. "You might be more comfortable if you sleep in these."

He straightened and took the clothes. "Thank you."

I took his suit pants, which he'd neatly laid flat on the bed. "I'll hang these up for you," I said as I walked back to his room, allowing him to get dressed in private and giving me a little distance to clear my head. My heart was pounding and my adrenaline was high. I was turned on, which I'm sure Shaun was very aware of. But I would stay true to my word.

When I went back to my room, Shaun was changed, though he looked just as sexy in his sleepwear. Almost. "You look more comfortable," I said, though I think he knew it was for my comfort, not his.

He smiled and turned to the bed. "I was unsure which side to turn down for you. I could assume from the book on the nightstand that this side is yours?" He gestured to the side closest to the door.

"Yes, but that's okay." I turned the overhead light off

and went to my side of the bed, which was the closest to the door, and switched on the lamp before pulling the covers back. I sat on the mattress, took my book, and slid my legs between the sheets.

Shaun studied my movements, then mimicked them on his side. The bed dipped with his weight but didn't jostle or jolt me. His movements were calculated and fluid; he made little or no impact on my surroundings, and I really did like that.

I also liked that he was in my bed.

His hair was natural and it flopped a little as he leaned his back against the headboard. He pulled the sheets up to the tops of his thighs and smiled when he caught me watching him.

He looked so incredibly human.

"Is this okay?" he asked.

I nodded. "Yes."

"You prefer older books," he observed.

I settled the paperback on my lap. "I do. I can appreciate electronic books, and I have many. But there's something about these old books that I love."

"What is it that you love?" he asked. There was a genuine interest in his eyes. Whereas past boyfriends had mocked my love of old books, Shaun showed only interest.

I picked the book up. "I love the weight of them, the smell of pages. And holding them, knowing there's an entire world inside. That's kind of lost in electronic books, for me at least."

Shaun smiled. "I was unaware that books had a scent."

Oh, of course. Although he was state of the art, androids didn't have olfactory senses. I lifted it to my nose and smelt it. "It smells of paper and printing, and dust and memories of my childhood, and escapism and happiness."

Shaun looked at the book, confused. "Though your description paints a lovely picture, I can only assume you speak metaphorically."

I laughed quietly. "Yes."

His gaze shot to mine. His sparkling blue eyes were intense, not with arousal but with something else. "The sound of your laughter appeals to me."

"Is that so," I said, not really asking.

He hummed, then he said, "I will refrain from disturbing you now so you can read your book."

Oh, right. The book...

"Yes," I said, picking it up again and making myself not look at him. And as I read, he didn't move. He remained utterly still. There was no fidgeting, no tossing, no turning, no grumbling at me to turn the light off.

It was lovely.

When my eyelids were too heavy to keep open, I closed the book and slid it onto the bedside table. I switched the light off and settled down into bed, and Shaun did the same. He lay flat on his back but his head turned to me. "You are sleepy," he murmured.

"Yeah."

"Goodnight, Lloyd. Pleasant dreams."

I smiled as I closed my eyes. "Goodnight, Shaun."

I REMEMBERED FEELING the sheet being pulled over me sometime in the middle of the night, and I remembered being aware that someone was in my bed, but I slept peacefully. And when I woke just before seven, I was on my side facing him. He lay there looking completely relaxed and patient. "Good morning," he said with a smile.

"Morning." God, he looked so damn good in my bed. A fact which didn't help my morning erection.

"You slept well," he said.

"I did."

"Shall I prepare your morning coffee?"

"I'll shower first," I said.

"Do you need any assistance with that?"

I fought a smile. "I can manage, thank you."

"Very well. What is on your agenda today?"

"I've taken vacation time from work to make sure your adjustment to living with me is smooth, so I don't need to go to work. I thought I could show you the apartment complex, how to leave, should you ever need to."

"Leave?" He blinked.

"In the case of a fire or another emergency." I rolled onto my back and scrubbed my hands over my face. "Just for your own safety."

"Very well."

I sat up, trying to palm my dick as inconspicuously as I could. "I won't be long in the shower. Please feel free to choose your clothes from your wardrobe." I stood and walked straight to my bathroom. I didn't mean to sound cold or like I was ordering him around. I just needed to get into the shower before I suggested we stay in bed.

Treat him like you would a human, I reminded myself. And with that in mind, I set the water to cold to douse any urgent desires. I couldn't deny the attraction, I just needed to set the pace. And if he were human and we were dating, yesterday would've been our first date, which made today our second. I could introduce more touching, possibly even kissing. Desire stirred in my belly despite the cold water.

Would I want to stop at kissing today? Would he want to? Should I take his desire and need for affection into

account, or as his custodian, did I know what was best
for him?

*Jesus. Stop overthinking it, Lloyd. Go with what feels
right.*

I shut off the water and quickly dried myself and
dressed for the day. I chose my usual casual clothes: navy
trousers and a knitted sweater. I'd been ridiculed most of
my life for my choice in clothes. Always too nerdy as a small
child and too uptight or preppy as an adult.

Whether being bullied—because I was a bookworm or
because I was gay—attributed to my OCD or caused it, no
one was sure. The many therapists I'd seen at my parents'
insistence when I was younger did nothing but tell me I was
broken, either outright or on a subconscious level, because
they were trying to "fix" me. Only broken things needed to
be fixed. But I wasn't broken. I didn't need to be fixed. I
needed to be understood.

And that was a difference no one could fathom. I didn't
want to be like them, I didn't want their definition of
normal. I wanted them to see the real me and to be okay
with it. Though no one ever did.

Except for Shaun.

He looked me up and down when I walked into the
kitchen. "You look very handsome today," he said.

He was standing at the coffee dispenser, and he was
wearing pants similar to mine, and a sweater. It helped that
I chose his wardrobe, so he could wear what I liked, and I
wondered if I'd taken away his choice.

"Thank you." I took the cup he offered. "Do you like the
clothes I bought you? Or would you prefer to choose your
own style?"

He blinked as though my question didn't compute with
his expected reasoning. "I like them very much."

"Well, just let me know if you'd prefer something different. I'm sure you can scan the internet for images of current fashions."

"I can. I can search any image you require, and I can search fashions for androids. But I like this aesthetic. I feel these clothes represent my importance to you."

His words took me by surprise. He wasn't just saying he liked them to please me. He understood my concern, and he understood me. I could have him wear nothing if I asked him to or wear a maid's costume outfit with crotchless underwear if that's what I so desired. But I didn't. I didn't want to *make* him do anything. I wanted him to be my equal.

"Yes, I guess they do." I sipped my coffee. "This is very good."

He grinned. "I am glad you like it. I studied the manual and best practices guide. Can I get you anything else?"

I shook my head slowly. "Not just yet."

"While you were sleeping, I performed a search-and-study on the book you were reading last night, so when you are finished, if you would like to discuss it, I will be more than happy to comply."

"I've read it many times." I sipped my coffee to hide my smile. "But I would like that, very much."

Shaun looked so peaceful, so composed, and so utterly perfect. "So, in your opinion," he started, "is Captain Ahab simply a character on an adventure, or is the white whale a metaphor for something more complex?"

And just like that, a thread in the fabric of my yearning for intellectual conversation pulled, and I smiled. I topped up my coffee and we spent the next several hours lost in conversation, discussing the literary depths of *Moby Dick*. At one point, I had the distinct realisation that I was in fact debating with an android, but the more he spoke, the tether of human/android distinction flittered away. I wasn't talking to an android, per se, I was simply talking to Shaun.

I was so lost in his extensive, well-rounded views—and he, seemingly, in mine—analysing the author's interpretation and meaning in diversity, class and social status, good and evil, and the existence of God, that something in my heart changed gears.

All I had ever wanted was someone I could talk to.

He appealed to me on so many levels; he was intelligent, composed, immaculately clean and tidy. And physically... well, physically, he was textbook perfect.

It wasn't until I needed to use the bathroom that I realised what time it was. It also explained why I was hungry. "My goodness, I didn't realise it was so late," I said.

"Allow me to get your lunch," Shaun said as I excused myself to the bathroom. I almost told him not to worry, and despite my anxiety that it might not be as neat as I'd like or presented as I would, I was curious as to what he would bring me.

When I came back to the living room, he stood beside his seat at the dining table, proudly displaying my lunch. There on a plate sat a sandwich, perfectly placed in the centre, aligned with precision. A water bottle sat on a coaster, again positioned perfectly at two o'clock to the plate.

He must've studied everything I'd done the day before to the millimetre. A human couldn't have done as good a job. *Perfect, perfect, perfect.*

"Does this please you?" he asked, his head tilted.

"Very much." I walked to him, took his hand, and gave it a squeeze. "Thank you."

I only let go of his hand when I sat down. He left his

hand on the table, and I had to marvel at the detail of his fingers. Perfectly manicured, creases at the knuckles, so very human.

He watched me eat. "You mentioned showing me the apartment complex," he said.

I swallowed my mouthful. "Yes. I was going to show you this morning but we got busy talking."

"Apologies if I monopolised your time."

"Oh no," I said quickly. "Talking with you today has been wonderful. I don't get to discuss books like that very often."

"Why not?"

"Because most humans I know find it boring. I can talk the basics for a little while, but even my colleagues—who are scholars in their own right—tire of it. They don't share my passion."

"I like it very much. It stimulates my neural networks to have such in-depth conversations with you."

My mouth went dry and I needed to sip my water so I could speak. "It stimulates something in me, as well."

His blue eyes fixed on mine. "Is your intellectual attraction a part of the dating ritual we are performing?"

My blood ran warm. "Yes."

"Your pupils dilate when you look at me like that. It tells me you are physically stimulated."

Oh boy.

"I am designed to mirror your stimulation. If you are aroused, I become aroused also."

God, how had I forgotten that?

"Sorry. I don't mean to... I'm sorry. If you're uncomfortable... I can't help it. It's been a long time for me and I find you very appealing."

"No need to apologise. When my tactile sensors and neural networks become stimulated, I find it pleasant."

I could feel my cheeks heat. "Pleasant?"

"Pleasing. Enjoyable." Then he whispered, "Pleasurable."

Oh boy, oh boy.

Was he flirting with me? Did androids flirt? Could they? Were they that advanced they could read social situations and behave in a manner to grant them the reward they sought? Did he long for my physical touch? Oh my God. Was he horny?

"Uh, how about we take that walk?" I said, taking my empty plate to the kitchen, quickly washing and drying it, then putting it away. *Everything in its place.* I grabbed my wallet and keys, just in case, and put my coat on at the front door.

Shaun stood and waited patiently. I couldn't see any pronounced bulge in his pants. Thank God. I knew from my research and the tour of the SATinc that the perma-semi-hard cock sat snug against the hip and only lengthened and protruded during sexual activity.

Great. Now I was thinking about his cock.

I went to open the door but stopped. "Uh, you'll need a coat."

"I do not feel the cold," he replied.

"No, but you'll look out of place without one," I explained. "People will notice you if you're underdressed."

"Oh."

"Not that I mind if people notice you," I added quickly. "I'd rather they didn't notice you because they think you're going to freeze to death."

He smiled as though something about my flustered demeanour amused him. "Very well."

"I'll grab you a coat." I dashed off to the hall, then realised I hadn't bought him a coat. I chose one of mine and took it out to him. I considered just handing it to him but thought he might appreciate my help. "Here," I said, holding it so he could slip an arm through.

"I am quite adept at dressing. I have excellent fine motor skills."

"I know. You dressed yourself this morning with buttons without my help." I grinned. "Helping someone into their coat is... a kind gesture. Something one might to do for his date."

Shaun's eyes glittered. "Then I accept your gesture," he said, sliding his arm into the sleeve of the coat.

"It's one of my jackets. I don't have one for you, so if you'd like, we can go shopping one day and you can pick one. If you want to, that is."

He fitted his other arm and I pulled on the collar to make it sit properly. His smile was one-sided, almost shy. It made my heart squeeze. "I would like that very much," he said, just above a whisper. As if he'd gauged my proximity and modified his voice to suit. Or maybe it was that flirting thing again.

I took a step back and let out a slow breath. I didn't know how long this no-physical rule of mine was going to hold out. This was technically our second date, after all...

He blinked and studied me for a second. "Are we waiting?"

"Oh, no," I said, opening the door. "I was just... thinking."

I waited for him to join me in the hall, then showed him our front door, or more importantly, the numbers beside it. "Our apartment is 35D."

"Thirty-fifth floor, apartment D," he clarified.

"That's correct." I nodded down the hall. "Lift's this way." We walked to it, and he watched as I pressed the button. "If there's a fire, you should take the stairs." I pointed to the exit sign above the stairwell. "But any other time, the lift is fine."

Shaun smiled like this new information, this little outing, was exciting.

The doors opened and we stepped inside. I showed him which button to press for the ground level and the basement car park. "If we walk somewhere, we go to G level. But if we drive somewhere, we go to B level." I showed him the other buttons on the panel he may need, the fire button, the emergency stop. I showed him the camera in the corner and explained it was a security apartment, that he'd need keys to get in and out.

He nodded, cataloguing everything. Then he looked behind us at the mirrored wall, just as the doors opened. "This way," I said, holding out my hand.

He took it without question, smiling as he looked around the foyer. It was a nice apartment building. Spacious, with elegant décor, and a reception desk which I walked toward.

"Good afternoon, Mr Salter," the android behind the counter said.

"Hello. I'd like to request a second security key for my apartment."

"Of course," he said. "One moment."

He retrieved the small token, swiped it, tapped on the screen, then handed it over. "Anything else I can do for you?"

"No, thank you."

He sat back down, and I noticed then that Shaun was

watching him with his head tilted slightly, a curious look in his eyes.

Oh, he was watching the other android.

"Come with me," I said, pulling gently on his hand. I led him to the front doors and out into the blustery Melbourne afternoon. The wind tousled his black hair and he looked even more striking in the natural daylight, even if it was overcast. His stark blue eyes, his straight nose, pink lips... He was gorgeous.

"Was that a B-Class android?" he asked.

"Yes." I watched for his reaction, but he kept still. "Do you have questions?"

He blinked. "Yes. Does the B-Class android have a name?"

"No. They don't. B- and C-Class androids don't. They have the same rights as all androids do, but they're addressed as simply *android*."

"Then why do A-Class androids have names?"

"Because you're a personal companion unit. For me to call you android would be impersonal." I frowned. "Do you like your name?"

He blinked again. "Shaun. Synthetic Human Android UNit."

"Yes. It's the name you had when I designed you. I never thought to change it. If you'd prefer me to call you by another name, you can choose one."

"I have no preference. I like it when you call me Shaun. I would rather not be called android."

"I'd never call you that. You have a name, and you are Shaun to me."

His lips twitched with the start of a smile. "Your hair is lifting," he said, looking at the top of my head.

I tried to pat it down but it was useless. "The wind," I explained. "Yours is doing the same."

His eyes went upward, but of course he couldn't see. I turned him around to look at the glass doors so he could see his reflection. He tilted his head again but said nothing.

We took a brief tour around the building and he was intrigued by it all. "Come on, it's getting cold," I said, leading him back toward the door. I handed him his key. "Swipe it near the keypad."

He did as I instructed and the doors opened. He smiled victoriously and we went inside, out of the blustery weather. I shook myself a little and fixed my hair. Shaun remained completely still. It really was only moments like that when I was reminded he wasn't human.

"Let's see if your key works in the lifts," I said, taking his hand again.

His hand was warm and felt lovely against mine. "You are cold," he stated.

"A little. It's winter, but we weren't outside for too long." We got to the lift, and when he swiped his key, the doors opened. "You press the buttons," I said.

He tapped the 35 button and the doors closed, but his eyes went to the mirror again. He looked at my reflection, then at his own. He tilted his head in that curious way he did, but he didn't smile.

It occurred to me he was having an existential moment.

I knew he was sentient. I knew he was aware, but I didn't know just how aware of his existence he was.

When the doors re-opened, I took his hand and walked him to our front door. His key worked just fine, and I suggested he leave it on the hall table near the door so he could grab it when he needed.

He placed the key down gently, then turned to me. I

wasn't exactly sure how to approach this, but I needed to say something.

"Shaun," I said gently. "Come with me." I held out my hand again and he took it quickly. He liked holding hands, and I had to admit, I liked it too. I led him to my room and took off my coat, then his. I hung them immediately, as I always did. Everything in its place.

Then I took him into my bathroom. The mirror was bigger in mine, so it made sense we came to mine. I stood, side by side with him, facing the mirror.

"Have you not seen yourself before?" I asked his reflection.

"No."

My heart sank a little. "I'm sorry. I should've thought about that before I took you out. I should have realised. I forgot about the mirror in the lift. To be honest, Shaun, I didn't even think of you not seeing yourself before or even your view or sense of self, and I feel as your custodian that I've let you down."

"You are not to blame," he said to my reflection. "It is not anyone's fault." Then he looked at himself for a moment. "We are different."

I smiled ruefully. "On the contrary, Shaun. We are very much alike."

"You are human, I am not."

"True. But we are still alike. Someone once told me that I was like an android, that I should date an android because humans don't meet my standards."

"Which standards are those?"

"I have... certain tendencies... compulsive tendencies for cleanliness. I like things done with precision and order. Humans tend to be... messy, and loud. I like silence."

He tilted his head. "If you like silence, would you rather I did not speak?"

"No, goodness no. Speaking is fine. Our conversations are wonderful." I let out a slow breath. "My ex-boyfriend would... I could hear him breathe and chew his food. It made me... uncomfortable and annoyed."

"Ex-boyfriend. A man with whom a person was once associated, in a relationship with."

"Yes. We dated for six months, and it was fine until he moved in with me." My brow furrowed at the memory. "He would leave his clothes on the floor. He would slurp his coffee, and I could hear him chew and swallow his food. He would snore. I found his cut toenails on the bathroom floor." I shuddered and took a breath and let it out slowly, trying to calm myself. "We were not compatible."

"Do all humans make these noises and leave toenail clippings on the floor?"

I cringed. "I hope not."

"And he told you to date an android?"

I nodded. "He meant it as an insult. That the only person who could possibly live with me would be someone who didn't need to breathe or eat." I lifted my chin and smiled at his reflection. "And you know what? He was right. I was hurt at first, but the more I thought about it, the more intrigued I was. It took me two years to find the courage to do it, but I'm very happy I did."

He did that half-smirk. "I am happy also."

I squeezed his hand and held our hands up so he could see them in the reflection, making him smile. "So, your sense of self," I started. "Do you have any questions about anything? Your creation, your design?"

"You chose my physical appearance?"

"Yes."

"Why is my hair black when yours is blond?"

"I chose your attributes for what I find intriguing. Dark hair and pale skin, blue eyes, have always been appealing to me."

"And my level of predesigned input on interests similar to your own?"

"Your level of intelligence and the ability to use the internet as a central processing unit, or your brain, is high, even for industry standards. You are an A-Class. There are not many like you. You're very special. And in regards to my interests, the company that designed and programmed you did so using my psychological and intelligence tests as a parameter, if you will. You were designed to be fully compatible for me, and me alone."

"And physically? Though I cannot determine visually through clothing, I assume anatomically we are similar. Was this by design also?"

I met his gaze, and as much as it scared me to do so, I refused to look away. "Yes. Would you like to see yourself?" I swallowed hard. "Without the clothing?"

His gaze went back to his reflection. "Yes."

Oh boy.

"Take off your sweater," I said, my voice a little shaky.

He looked down at our joined hands. "I will need my hand back," he said, repeating my line from yesterday back to me.

I laughed. "Touché." I let go of his hand and he adeptly pulled his sweater off.

It messed up his hair a little, in a very adorable, human way, and he smiled when he saw his hair in the reflection. "Wind and sweaters have a similar effect on hair."

I chuckled. "They do."

He combed his fingers through it and looked to me. "Is that better?"

But I couldn't stop looking at his chest, at his arms. Every line and plane, every defined hill and valley of muscle was like he was a sculpted work of art, a masterpiece in anatomy. His chest was broad, his nipples darker and pebbled. His ribs were shadowed and his abs were flat and tight. I'd asked for a swimmer physique and he was... utterly perfect.

"You like what you see," he said. It wasn't a question. There was no doubt. If he could detect pupil dilation and elevated heart rate, there was no point in denying it.

"Yes."

So he unbuttoned his trousers and undid the fly. The sound of the zipper almost brought the tenuous hold on my will undone.

The material slid down his well-defined thighs and puddled around his calves, and he slid his fingers underneath the elastic of his briefs. I wanted to tell him to leave them on, that my strength of will could only take so much. I could already see the outline of his cock, snug against his hip, and it made my mouth water. I didn't want to take advantage of him, but this wasn't about me. It was about him having a true sense of self.

He needed to see all of himself.

He slid his briefs down and I dry swallowed on reflex.

Oh boy.

I tried to keep my eyes on his face. I tried, but when I looked at the reflection, I could see all of him.

Oh. Boy.

Freed from his underpants, his cock hung heavy, thick and semi-hard. Cut with a beautiful head, there were even veins, and his balls hung heavy, nestled in a short thatch of dark hair. So God help me, my knees went weak.

"You like what you see," he said, his voice lower, seductive.

All I could do was nod.

"Do you want to touch me?"

My gaze shot to his. "I want you to be comfortable, and I want you to want me to touch you."

"I do want you to touch me."

Holy hell.

"I can tell when you are aroused, Lloyd," he murmured. It boomed like surround sound in the tiled bathroom, as if he whispered in both my ears. "And it makes me aroused. I was designed to be aroused when you are. You designed me that way, yet you abstain."

It took me a few attempts to speak. "I... I uh... I want to make sure you're ready and understand the significance of what we do."

"I understand. I can quote you every reference to consent and willingness there is on the internet. I can reference the importance of sexual communication between partners and what it means to give one's body to someone else. I can recall any information you desire. Which, in particular, do you want me to know?"

"I want you to want it. I want you to know that if I take you to bed, if we further our physical relationship, what that means for you. As a person."

"I'm not a person."

"As a sentient being. With desires and needs."

"I desire you to touch me. Yet you will not."

And there it was. Pure and simple.

"You desire?"

"Desire. As in a strong feeling of wanting to have something or wishing for something to happen."

"I know what it means," I replied, my voice barely a breath.

"Do you not have desires?"

"I do." I almost laughed. "I really do."

"Am I not what you designed? Is something inadequate?"

I turned quickly to face him, and he turned to me. "You are more than adequate. You are a new definition of perfect." I put my hand to his cheek, marvelling in his warmth. "I need a better word than perfect."

"Faultless. Flawless. Impeccable."

"Better than those. You are even better than those."

"Pluperfect," he said.

I chuckled. "Well, it doesn't quite have a nice ring to it. I think I just like Shaun. I think your name should now mean better than perfect."

I moved my hand to his jaw, feeling the smoothness, the hardness. Then I swiped my thumb across his bottom lip, gasping at how real it felt. His gaze narrowed, his lips parted a little more.

"May I kiss you?" I asked, barely audible.

He nodded, so I licked my lips, and still cupping his face, I pulled him in a little and leaned in further so I could ghost my lips across his.

His eyes closed.

Oh my God, he closed his eyes.

So I pressed my lips to his a little harder, but still soft so he could feel it. It was his first kiss. I wanted it to be perfect. I brought my other hand to his neck and tilted my head just a fraction. I opened his mouth with mine and let my tongue touch his.

I'd seen enough research to know he could kiss, and when I'd designed him, Sasha had shown me how all body parts worked.

I pulled his lower lip between mine and reluctantly ended the kiss.

Shaun took a second to open his eyes, and it looked as though it took him half a second to focus on me.

"Was that okay?" I asked.

"I would appreciate very much if we could do that again."

I chuckled again, then looked down at his cock. "Uh, maybe we should do it again but with clothes on. Or I might end up rushing you through sex-ed class."

"I know all sexual education data. And I have detailed programming on the art of gay lovemaking."

I laughed louder this time and took a step back. "My self-control is barely holding by a thread. But that's good to know."

He quickly pulled up his underpants and trousers, then fastened the fly. I had to admit, I found it a little easier to breathe once he'd done that.

I handed him his sweater and he pulled it on over his head. His dexterity was remarkable. "Here," I said. "Let me fix your hair." I gently combed my fingers through his dark strands. They were soft and silken. Real. I looked his hair over. "There. Perfect."

He was watching me with an unfamiliar look in his eyes. "Thank you." Then he glanced at the mirror, at himself, then at my reflection.

"Are you okay?" I asked, puzzled.

He paused, which was odd. "I believe so."

That was odd too. "Shaun? Do you have something you'd like to ask?"

"I wish to do more kissing."

I laughed and let out a nervous breath. "Okay, I concede. I was hoping to pace our physical interaction, but you're rather persistent." It wasn't even that he was persistent. It was pretty clear my hesitance to further our sex life was confusing to him. I stepped over to the basin and leaned my arse against it, then motioned for him to come to me. "I want you to initiate this kiss. If you have extensive research data, teach me."

He smirked and stood in front of me, his eyes fixed on mine. He put a hand on my waist, his other hand to my jaw, then he slowly pressed against me. His entire front to mine, his cock against my hip.

Oh boy.

He was all hard planes and muscle, strength but tender and gentle.

Then he brushed his nose to mine, his lips. An almost kiss at first, then harder, deeper. His tongue extended into my mouth, and the hand on my waist went around my back and he pulled us closer together while pushing me against the basin.

He didn't just kiss me. He damn well owned me in that kiss.

I slid my hands around his back, over his arse, and pulled our hips together, rubbing my hard-on against him. His cock felt bigger at my hip and I realised he was turned on because I was. I groaned at the thought.

While he had no need for oxygen—he could kiss indefinitely—I was breathless.

Which meant he could also have sex indefinitely.

I pulled my mouth away, reluctantly and gasped for air. "Wow."

He looked smug but much happier now. "You are aroused," he whispered.

I barked out a laugh but kept his hips locked with mine. "You feel really good."

He cupped my face. His smooth hands were warm, as was the look in his eyes. "I wish to have sex now."

I barked out a laugh. Maybe it was a groan. He wanted it; I wanted it. Why was I so hesitant? I didn't want to take advantage of him but he was offering. Asking. "Not in here," I said. "Your first time won't be in a bathroom."

I took his hand and led him to my bedroom. I turned and pulled him against me so I could kiss him again, and he didn't mind at all. I pulled his sweater over his head, breaking our kiss. Then I undid his pants and slid my hands inside his briefs and over his arse, pushing them down. "Sit on the bed," I whispered.

He did, so I knelt between his legs and undid his shoes and pulled his socks off. His feet were so very lifelike, incredibly detailed, and clean. I kissed the inside arch of his foot and let it fall so I could kiss up his thigh. The texture of his skin was incredible. My God, he was so unbelievably real.

I pulled his clothes off and stood up. He sat there and watched as I undid my pants, then each button on my shirt. I let the shirt fall off my shoulders to the floor, then toed out of my shoes. Shaun's eyes fixed on the bulge in my briefs and I ran my hand over it, revelling in the friction, in the attention, before I pulled the material down over my hips.

"Lie down on the bed," I said, my voice rough. He did as I asked, his amazing body laid out like a banquet, just for me. I took the lube from my dresser and threw it beside him.

I crawled up the bed, taking in the details of his balls, his cock. He was fully extended now; his arousal matched mine. Literally. "I'm going to lick you," I warned, then flattened my tongue and drew it up his shaft.

"Oh," he said. "Oh my."

I smiled and did it again, licking around the tip. It was, for all intents and purposes, a dildo. A very, very lifelike, seven-and-a-half-inch dildo. Perfectly sculptured, veins in all the right places, flushed pink at the tip. But it wasn't a dildo exactly. It was Shaun's cock, and it had sensors that told his processing unit what felt good and, as I'd seen in the video research I'd done, it would pulse when he climaxed.

"I'm not going to penetrate you," I said, then tongued his cockhead. "But I want to make you come."

"Oh," he groaned. He actually groaned.

I looked up at him and he had his head back. "Look at me when I do this to you," I said.

His head shot up and he locked eyes with mine as I slipped my lips over his cock.

"Does that feel good?"

"Yes."

"Can you come like this?"

"I reach my climax when you do."

As soon as he said it, I remembered. He would come when I did, but I didn't know he could *only* come when I did. As much as I wanted him to have free will, something about that appealed to me. Only I could make him come. Yes, I liked that a lot.

I leant back on my haunches, my own cock jutting out, desperate for attention.

I was so tempted to slick him up and sink inside him.

So, so very tempted.

But another time. Next time, even. I wanted his first time to be about him. So I took the lube and poured it up his length. "This is lube, it makes it feel slippery."

I leaned over him, aligned our cocks, and took them both in one hand. His heavy-lidded eyes shot open and his lips parted, so I leaned down and kissed him, and he groaned again. The sound was delicious and obscene, and I didn't realise that sex noises were included, but I was ever grateful they were.

Taking my weight on one hand, I wanted to watch his face as I gave him his first orgasm. And my God, he felt so good. Too good. His cock sliding against mine, slick and hard in my fist, so utterly perfect.

It had been so long since I'd been intimate with anyone, and I'd been so turned on by him since he got here, I knew I wouldn't last long. "You're gonna make me come," I grunted between thrusts.

He put his hands on my hips and rocked harder against me. My rhythm faltered, my breath hitched, and I thrust harder, chasing the peak. "God, Shaun."

His mouth fell open and his eyes went wide as we came. I arched against him and he rolled his hips. I shot my release onto his stomach and his cock pulsed in my hand, against my cock, sending my climax to new heights.

"Oh God," I cried. "Yes. Yes!"

Shaun's back arched off the mattress before he slumped back onto it. He blinked, once, twice, then ever so slowly, he smiled.

I collapsed on top of him, out of breath and completely spent. He ran his hands from my hips to my back and he held me there.

"Your heart rate is erratic."

I chuckled. "Yes. Sex will do that." I pulled back to look at his face. "Did you like that?"

"Very much. I'd like to do it again."

I laughed and kissed him, amazed at how natural it felt to do that. "Well, humans need a little recovery time."

He smirked. "But you will do it again?"

I rolled my eyes. He'd already won. It was a battle I'd tried to fight, but he'd defeated me easily. "Yes. I was trying to pace our sexual introductions but—" I kissed him again, smiling. "—you looked at me with those blue eyes and said you wanted it. I couldn't deny you."

"My blue eyes?"

I nodded and kissed him again. "I'm very attracted to you." I looked at his eyes. His pink lips were wet and slightly parted. "You're very good at kissing."

"I was designed for it. For you."

"Yes, you were."

"My mouth was also designed to take your erection," he said.

Oh boy. I let my head fall to his neck and it took me a moment to find the ability to speak. "That's good to know."

"Does that embarrass you?" he asked.

"A little. People don't often discuss sexual acts or abilities with such candour."

"Should I not say such things to you?"

Oh boy. We needed to be honest with each other, but I didn't want him to discuss fellatio or climaxing like he'd mention the blue sky if we were out somewhere. "How about we can discuss things openly in this bedroom?" I suggested. "Or if we're alone and you have a question, you could ask me if it's an appropriate time?"

He gave a small nod. "Very well."

I pulled back a little to find I was stuck to him with my smeared come. "We should get you cleaned up," I said. Then I remembered that Myles had said Shaun would like it if I helped him. "Would you like me to help you clean up? I can run you a shower."

His answer was immediate. "Yes."

I rolled off him and got off the bed, and Shaun did the same. But before I could walk away, he took my hand, stopping me. "Lloyd," he said softly.

I looked at him. "Yes?"

"I wish to kiss you again. Right now, if I may?"

His words shocked me. Some moments I could easily forget he was an android. He was so very humanlike in almost everything he did. But then moments like this would strike me as odd. He *was* an android. He wasn't human, so why did he act like one? Did all A-Class personal companion units have wishes and physical needs? But before I could wonder any more, or even ask, he slid his hand along my jaw and pulled me in for another kiss. He was slower this time, more tender, and he finished by resting his forehead against mine.

"Will you be joining me in the shower?" he whispered.

Oh boy.

CHAPTER FIVE

"YOU CAN ACTIVATE the shower by pressing this button. It's set to a standard forty-five degrees Celsius." I pointed to the control panel on the shower wall in his bathroom and waited for him to press it.

The water shot from the wall jets, and Shaun's smile widened, though he extended his hand. "After you."

I walked into the long shower cubicle. It was simply three walls, completely tiled, no glass panelling, with water jets down two walls and overhead. I put my head back and let the water massage my head, my back, and my chest, and when I opened my eyes, Shaun stood there, staring at me.

"You are more appealing when you are wet," he said.

I laughed and held out my hand. He took it and I pulled him into the shower, giving him the line of the water jets. I took the soap recommended for his skin and put it in his hand. "This soap is especially for you. You rub this all over your body."

"I am not certain that is a task with which I'm familiar," he said. "Perhaps you should do it for me."

I chuckled in disbelief and shock. "Is that so?"

He smirked.

"I thought you had extensive knowledge about... everything."

The water had flattened his hair, which now lay in spikes down his forehead. His blue eyes sparkled with humour and daring, and water cascaded off his chin. "Some things are best shown."

My God. He was truly flirting. Not even flirting. He was feigning ignorance of a life skill I was completely certain he knew how to do on his own so that I would touch him all over.

He was being provocative. Playing with sexual innuendo and manipulating me to give him what he wanted. I might have been a little perturbed if he hadn't been wet and naked, smiling like that, and semi-hard, offering me his body.

I knew once this gate to sexual interaction had been opened, it wouldn't ever close. Once I'd started, I wouldn't want to ever stop.

"Lean your shoulders back against the wall," I said, my voice gruff with desire.

His smirk became a smile, and he did what I asked, letting his arms hang at his sides. The water jets hit his ribs and chest and when I rubbed the soap over his chest, he closed his eyes and hummed. "It is recommended I be cleaned after every sexual encounter," he said in a murmur.

I soaped up my hand, pumped his cock, and cupped his balls, washing him thoroughly. "Is that so?"

His eyes opened lazily, heavy lidded. He looked from my eyes to my cock, then back to my eyes. God, now he was being seductive? "May I touch you?"

"No," I said, asserting my authority. He kept his hands by his sides. I stood over him, my feet outside his, our cocks aligned. Being with him in the shower and having him be so sexual, I was ready to go again—which he obviously was in tune with.

He would be as aroused as I was.

I leaned against him, pressing our erections between our bellies, and brushed my lips to his. "You like being touched," I whispered.

"Yes."

"You like being kissed."

"Yes."

"You like to come."

He flexed his hips but kept his hands by his sides. "Yes."

"Do you want to touch me?"

"Yes."

I rutted against him, chasing our release. He would come whenever I did. I put my hands on his hips, up over his flat stomach, his lats, his pecs, his nipples. I used this opportunity to explore his body, every inch, every soft edge and hard plane. He felt incredible.

He might have been an android, but he was all man.

I crushed my mouth to his and he opened, letting me in. His tongue flicked mine, teased and tangled, and he moaned.

God help me, the sounds he made sent me hurtling toward the precipice.

I reached between us and took both of us in my fist again. His arms remained still, following my order, and there was something heady about that. Something that sang to the control freak in me.

I looked down between us, at our cocks together, and a jolt of pleasure shot through me, my orgasm rocketed through me. Shaun pulsed in my hand and ecstasy crashed through me as I came. Shaun's cock pulsed again, and he groaned as I shot between us, my come quickly washing away with the stream of water.

I fell against him for a breathless moment, and when I opened my eyes and looked at his face, he was staring intently at me. "May I touch you now?"

I rolled my neck, languid and boneless. "Yes, please."

He quickly wrapped his arms around me, caging me in but cradling me gently, and he pressed me against the wall. I was barely jostled; he was so aware of space and pressure, but his weight against me felt divine, hard in all the right places, yet his lips were so soft.

He initiated this kiss. He wanted it. He ran his hands into my hair, down my back, and over my arse, touching me everywhere he could reach while he still kissed me. And when he pulled away, he cupped my jaw before kissing me softly again, his eyes closed.

"I like showering very much," he said.

I laughed and reached up to shut the water off. My chest was still heaving and my mind was swimming, my body spent and blissful. I kept one hand on his hip, keeping him right where he was.

It was ridiculous. I'd climaxed twice and it still wasn't enough. Admittedly, it had been a long time for me. I'd rarely even touched myself since Ian left. In the last two years, I'd had no real desire and the mess was never worth the relief.

But it was different with Shaun.

I was attracted to him. My body reacted to him. I shivered, causing him to pull back. "You are cold."

"Not really." I groaned and stood up straight, ignoring my cock for now. "My body likes being naked with yours."

Shaun smiled, looking rather dishevelled with his wet hair unbrushed. "I like it very much also."

Reluctantly, I walked out of the shower and grabbed a towel, handing him one too. "Yes well," I said, drying my hair. "I fear that we may do little else, now we've started."

"I have no objections to that," he replied, drying himself.

"So, you can dry yourself, yet you required help in washing yourself?" I asked, trying not to smile.

"One can never be too cautious when it comes to cleanliness," he answered, not even trying to hide his smirk. He held out his towel, and his eyes sparkled with mischief. "If you would like to ensure I am adequately dry, you may do it yourself."

I huffed out a laugh and tied my towel off around my waist. "I wasn't aware being provocative was in your programming."

He dried himself off and neatly hung the towel on the rack. Then he turned back to me, completely naked. His glorious cock and balls hung heavy, distracting my attention. I had to make myself look at his face. He almost smiled. "Playful and suggestive banter is encouraged, is it not?"

"Clothes are also encouraged."

"If you insist."

My gaze fell to his cock once more and that familiar stirring began low in my belly. Surely twice was enough in one day. My eyes flickered back to his. "Yes. I insist. I'll grab your clothes for you. We left them in my room."

After we'd stripped before falling into bed, I added mentally.

I found our clothes exactly where we'd left them. Which was very unlike me. Normally I would never be so reckless with placement. Everything had a place and the floor was not it. Even with Ian, when we undressed for bed, I would always carefully fold and rehang our clothes.

I quickly pulled on my trousers and shirt, then took Shaun's back to him. He was standing at his bathroom mirror, brushing his hair. But that wasn't what caught my attention. It was the briefs I'd bought for him.

He looked down at them. "Are these too small? There is less material coverage in this pair than the last."

I breathed out slowly and swallowed hard. And oh no, they weren't too small at all. His bulge barely fit, the white material stretched across the ridgeline of his cock, and showed off his arse better than any underwear ad I'd ever seen. "No, they're the perfect size."

"You like them on me," he said. My gaze shot to his and he smiled. "Your pupils dilated and your lips parted, involuntary responses to sexual attraction."

I closed my eyes and let out a slow breath. "You should put these on or I'll take you back to my bedroom." I put his clothes on the basin. "I'll be in the kitchen when you're dressed."

I left him there and went in search of dinner. I hadn't realised the whole afternoon had passed. It was dark outside, and that meant we'd soon be going to bed, and oh boy... I was pretty sure I'd be buried inside him later tonight.

"Is everything all right?" Shaun asked.

He startled me. I had my hands on the kitchen counter, my head down, eyes closed, trying to catch my breath. I shot up straight. "Yes, yes. Everything is fine."

He was dressed now, his hair brushed neatly. He looked so handsome, almost like a mannequin; so different from his straggly wet hair and sexy smirk in the shower. It was hard to reconcile the two.

"This time yesterday, you had eaten your evening meal," Shaun said, going to the fridge. "Allow me to get it for you." He took out a small premade meal. "Chicken, vegetables, and rice. Does this sound appealing?"

Okay, so he'd dropped the sexual provocation and flirting and was back to being the overt professional. I didn't know if I was relieved or disappointed.

"Yes, it sounds fine, thank you."

He placed it in the oven, then set the table. "Please sit," he offered with a slight bow of his head. "I shall bring it to you."

I sat in my seat, and a moment later, he placed my dinner in front of me, and a glass of water. Everything was perfectly positioned, aligned, and in order. Then he sat in his seat and tilted his head. "Is something incorrect?" He studied my plate and glass, as if gauging angles and distances from the edges of the table, then finding them exactly right, he looked back up at me.

"No, everything is fine," I answered. "I just..."

"You just what?"

I sipped my water. "I just wondered how you can switch between being sexually suggestive and inviting to being... formal."

"Formal?"

"Professional," I explained, though that really wasn't the right word either. "As in, in the bedroom and bathroom, you're flirty and seductive, and now you're all serious."

"Please eat your dinner before it goes cold," he said, a smile curling at the edges of his lips. He spoke while I ate. "I refrained from sexual banter with you because I sensed your unease. You were uncomfortable in my bathroom when you told me to dress, saying you will take me to your bedroom as if it was a bad thing. I sensed your need for restraint, and so I restrained. Did I read you wrong?"

I swallowed down my mouthful. "No. You didn't. I was uncomfortable... well, I was... I find you very attractive," I admitted again, this time more weakly. "And I fear now that we've become physical, it'll be all we will be, and I want more than that with you."

"I enjoyed being physical with you, very much. Sexual acts are so much more fulfilling in practice than in theory."

I chuckled as I chewed my food. "Yes, they are."

"But Lloyd, I am equally rewarded with intellectual discussions as I am by sexual intercourse. I am programmed for both. If you wish to discuss the iambic pentameter of Shakespeare's sonnets, I will happily oblige. Or the power and limit of logic and objectivity and value theories from your philosophy classes. Or the realism and radicalism of modern ethics in philosophy. I am quite well versed in all subjects."

I finished my dinner and sipped my water. "Equally rewarded?"

"I find both equally stimulating. One stimulates my social parameters of intellect and world knowledge. The other stimulates my physical sensors. I require both."

Now it was me who tilted his head. "You require both?"

"Yes. To maintain health and optimum performance levels."

"You require sex?"

"It is not a requirement. Touch, hand-holding, hugging, all send positive messages to my processing unit. As does conversation and debating subjects of choice." He looked a little puzzled. "This was not assumed knowledge?"

"Well, yes... and no," I answered lamely because he looked even more perplexed. "I mean, they told me you would like conversations and intellectual interaction and you would like physical interaction."

"But you did not believe them?"

In hindsight, when they told me, I was so caught up on his physical appearance, I wasn't sure I thought anything... "I'm not sure. May I ask you something?"

"Of course."

"Now that you've had both intellectual and physical interaction, which do you prefer? You said you find them both equally stimulating, but which felt better?"

"Your question is subjective and biased to one answer. The word 'feel' is synonymous with physical, is it not?"

I smiled, liking he questioned my phrasing. I liked being challenged. "It can be. Figuratively speaking. So let me ask again; if I were to ask you to choose between debating literary history and philosophy or going back to my bed, which would you rather?"

His smile was slow spreading, his eyes glittered with temptation. But then he replied, "Both. I would suggest we discuss literary topics for an hour or so. Then when you wish to retire for the evening, I could accompany you to your bed and you could... stimulate my proprioceptive and exteroceptive sensors." He held my gaze and his left eyebrow raised, just a fraction. "Several times if you are able."

Oh boy.

WE DID DISCUSS MORE LITERATURE. His fascination with *Moby Dick*'s Ishmael drove two hours of characterisation breakdown and analysis and if the subversive subtext was the author's intention or the reader's interpretation.

Whether Shaun's viewpoint honestly differed from mine or if he chose to disagree so we could debate at length, I wasn't sure. I didn't much care. Because it was a subject I could talk about forever, and I'd never met anyone who felt the same.

After Shaun quoted references from American literary professors to back his claim, he finished with, "I am not even convinced his name is Ishmael."

"What?" I shook my head. "How can you not be convinced? He says it is."

"No, he says, 'Call me Ishmael,' as though it is a persona he has adopted and is clearly another Biblical reference. Ishmael from the Bible was an outcast, ostracised and dismissed by his family in favour of a half-brother. Is it not reasonable to assume the character in the book says 'Call me Ishmael' as a way of identifying himself, not by his name, but how he sees himself?"

I didn't know whether to pull my hair out, scream at the ceiling, or kiss him.

I settled for smiling instead. I walked over to where Shaun sat and he looked expectantly up at me. Then, putting one knee beside his, then my other, I straddled him. His head tilted back as he kept eye contact, a smile pulled at his lips. "Do you wish to keep discussing the book? Or is this a way to concede I may be correct?"

I scoffed, unable to stop the grin. "I will concede yours is a fair argument, but I wouldn't go as far as to say correct." I kissed him, pulling his bottom lip between mine. "But I'm done discussing books."

He put his hands on my hips and I rocked down on him.

His erection matched mine. "Does debating literature at such length arouse you?" he asked.

I couldn't tell if he was joking or not. "Maybe I'm not too different from you," I whispered against his lips, grinding down on his cock. "Maybe I need both too."

He pulled my hips down, rubbing me against his hard-on, and I kissed him deep and thoroughly. Then I remembered what he said about his mouth.

His throat was fitted with a Fleshjack sleeve...

I broke the kiss and gasped a breath. "I think we should go to my room."

He gripped my hips firmly and stood up, holding me in place. His strength and tenderness were an incredible juxta-position. I chuckled and wrapped my legs around him, kissing him again, and he carried me to my room where he gently lowered me to the bed.

He stood before me. "How do you want me?" he whis-pered so dirty it curled around my insides.

"I want you to open your mouth and take me inside."

He gave me that one-sided smirk that made my heart skip a beat. "Shall I undress for you?"

I considered telling him to stay clothed but figured his glorious body should be on display at every opportunity. "Yes."

He looked down and started to unbutton his shirt, and when he lifted his head, his eyes were heavy lidded and full of heat.

It made my cock throb.

I remained silent and still and watched him. His shirt slid off his shoulders like silk, then he stared at me while he undid his trousers and slowly undid the zipper. *God, was he putting on a show for me?*

I let out a low breath and licked my lips. I wanted to

palm myself but restrained. *It'll be better to wait for him to do it*, I told myself.

He let his trousers slide down his thighs, and a smile played at his lips, a teasing smile.

"And your briefs," I said, my voice low and husky.

He obeyed and his cock sprang forward, fully erect. But then he turned around and bent over to undo his shoelaces, giving me a very deliberate, very glorious view of his arsehole. A flawless, small hole that stretched open without preparation, ribbed for ultimate pleasure.

Oh boy.

"Are you teasing me?" I asked with a smile.

He straightened and turned to face me. "Yes."

"I want to try your mouth first," I said.

"It would be my pleasure," he whispered. "How do you want me?"

"Sit on the bed, lean your back against the headboard."

He stepped out of his trousers and sat on the bed, then scooted up till his back was against the headboard. His cock jutted proudly upward and it made my mouth water, so, fully dressed, I threw the lube beside him and crawled onto the bed, up his legs. Then, with my eyes on his, I leaned down and licked him, from base to tip.

His mouth formed an O and his back arched a little. I would definitely be doing that again soon, but right now I had more pressing needs.

Moving up onto my knees, I straddled him, almost pressing my hips against his chest, and undid my fly. He looked up at me with imploring blue eyes, his mouth slightly open. I pulled out my cock, already slick with precome, and applied some lube.

He watched intently, obviously learning for next time, and put his hands on my thighs. He curled his fingers around to the backs of my legs and pulled me forward so my cockhead sat on his bottom lip. It was such an erotic sight.

"Open wider," I murmured.

He did, looking up at me, then with his hands on my legs, he slowly pulled me into his mouth. I brushed up against the opening at the back of his mouth, pushed and breached the hole, sliding in as far as I could.

"Oh my God," I breathed. It was so tight, so slick, and warm, and ribbed, and made just for me.

He groaned, the vibration sending jolts of pleasure through me. I rested my forehead against the wall, trying to quell the need to thrust and come, taking a second to breathe.

But it was no use. He felt too damn good.

I leaned back and looked down, his eyes were closed and my cock disappeared between his lips, my balls on his chin. There was something empowering, something neat and clean, about being fully clothed when he was naked. "So beautiful," I murmured.

His eyes opened and looked up at me, full of lust and heat. With his hands still around my thighs, he pushed me back an inch or two, then pulled me back in. It set off a reaction I was powerless to stop; I needed to fuck, I needed to come.

I took hold of the headboard and began to thrust. Shaun gripped my legs and groaned, and I knew he felt as turned on as me.

He was programmed to come when I did. And I was so close, which meant he was too. Then, like he needed more, like he was desperate to come, he gripped my arse and pulled me deeper into his throat.

"Oh, God!" I cried out as my blinding orgasm rocketed through me. With every muscle in my body strung tight, every nerve ending alight with pleasure, I came and he groaned as he came too.

I couldn't stop rocking into him, he felt so, so good. His grip on my arse loosened a little and his lips curled up in a smile around my cock. He slow-blinked, and his entire face looked so serene, in what could only be described as bliss.

I reluctantly pulled out and slumped on him, spent and boneless. He scooped me up in his arms and rolled us over, cradling me gently, so we could lie down and hold each other. He held me close, my face nestled in his neck, and I tightened my hold on him too, and for the longest moment— a most perfect moment—we didn't move.

I almost dozed off, but then I remembered he'd need to be cleaned. It could have ruined the moment, but I realised this was part of who we were now. If he were human, I'd want to take care of him, and this was no different. I pulled back so I could see his face. He still looked serene, impossibly handsome, dishevelled, and sated. I traced my thumb along the lube on his bottom lip. It looked like gloss, and I said, "We should get you cleaned up."

He nodded and smiled. "Thank you."

He was thanking me? "What for?"

"For what we just did. I liked it very much."

Oh. I ducked my head and chuckled. "I liked it very much too."

He lifted my chin and thumbed my cheek. "Why do you blush?"

"I don't know," I fibbed.

He tilted his head. "You spoke so brazenly when you wanted me to open my mouth, but now you are embarrassed."

I considered lying again but stopped myself. There was such clarity in his striking blue eyes, it compelled me to be honest. "I didn't just like what we did just now," I whispered, cupping his face. "I loved it. I love the conversations we have. I love that you understand my need for neatness and order. You get me, like no human ever has."

He blinked. "Love. A strong feeling of affection."

I stared at him, reality hitting me hard in the chest. I could very well be falling for him, but he would never reciprocate. He couldn't. He had a programmed understanding of human emotions and could synthetically empathise. But he would never feel it for himself. He would never love me back.

My heart squeezed and sank like a stone.

"Yes, that's correct," I whispered. I rolled out of his arms and walked into my bathroom. "I'll start the shower."

CHAPTER SIX

I WOKE up to find myself wrapped around Shaun. I sighed contentedly and smiled as I stretched, and he traced his fingers through my hair. "Good morning," he said.

And then I remembered my epiphany last night...

I was falling for someone who could never love me back.

I pulled away and scrubbed my hands over my face.

"Is everything okay?" he asked.

I risked a glance at him, then rolled over and sat up on the edge of the bed. "Yes, of course. I'm just... I'm just going to have a shower."

I got up and closed the bathroom door behind me, walking right into the shower and hitting the water button. The hot water kneaded my neck and shoulders, ran over my head, and it did make me feel a little better. The ache in my chest wouldn't be so easily fixed.

I should've known this was possible, and I really should've known better. I don't know why I didn't think it was possible, even before I'd decided to get him. I'd researched everything. I'd done my due diligence about responsibility, finances, longevity. I knew what to expect with everything. Everything!

Everything except this.

I knew people became attached to their androids, and I expected this. I expected us to become friends, and I expected to get used to cohabiting, and I even expected to become close to him.

But I didn't expect love.

I scrubbed my hair and washed every inch of my body. And then I did it again.

Would it be so terrible if he could never love me back?

He would be forever loyal. He would be attuned to only me. Forever. Was that not love to him? Was that not the synthetic equivalent?

I let my head fall back into the stream of hot water and took a deep, cleansing breath.

It would have to be enough.

I would make it be enough.

I shut off the water and dried myself, shaved, and dressed for the day. I found him in the kitchen, holding my coffee mug out to me. And the second he saw me, he smiled. Not just a polite smile, but a genuinely happy-to-see-me smile. "You are dressed very smartly today. Are you going somewhere important?"

"I'm not," I said, taking a sip of coffee. It was exactly as I liked it. "We are."

He tilted his head just a fraction. "We?"

"Yes. I thought you might like to buy a coat today."

He brightened. "Oh, yes. I would like that. Shall I get dressed?"

I looked down at his sleep pants and the fact he wasn't wearing a shirt. I hid my smile behind my coffee. "I like this look, very much. In fact, you could wear nothing but your underwear and I wouldn't mind one bit. But people at the shopping centre might stop and stare."

His lips quirked. "Facetious. Treating serious issues with deliberately inappropriate humour. To be flippant."

I laughed. "I like your sense of humour."

Shaun closed the small distance between us and took my coffee, holding it out to the side in one hand, cupping my face with his other. He leaned in and kissed me before smirking again. "I like yours as well."

He gave me back my coffee and walked out, disappearing down the hall to his room.

I like yours as well, he'd said. He liked my sense of humour. And yesterday he said he didn't want me to call him android, as if his preference signified a strong dislike. If he could like something or dislike something, then why could he not love something?

What exactly were the parameters on his synthetic emotions?

I took out the control panel and scrolled through the settings, looking for the section under Social Intelligence. Shaun had the ability to recognise and interpret, process and simulate emotions, as I was told in the SATinc office the day I designed him. So he *could* simulate emotions...

It was some in-depth and complex information. One I probably needed a degree in robotics engineering to begin to understand. I really should read through the whole information manual I was given. I'd been so busy treating him like a new and shiny toy, I'd neglected to learn about him first.

Shaun came back out and sat down on the sofa next to me, straight-backed and a little concerned when he saw what I was reading. "Is there something I can help you with? I can answer any question you have."

I slid my hand into his to reassure him. "I know you can.

But I should also read everything to help me understand you better. I'd hate to think I was neglecting anything."

"You are not neglecting anything," he replied. "In fact, the stimulation you provide is more than adequate."

I smiled. "You're very complex, Shaun, and I want to know everything there is to know. How to treat you better."

He smirked and raised one eyebrow ever so slightly. "The only way you could treat me better would be to take me to your bedroom."

Now I chuckled. "You certainly do have desires, don't you." It wasn't a question.

"Yes. You could also read one of your favourite books to me. I would enjoy that very much also."

I looked up at him, and though he smiled, there was a tightness to his eyes. "Shaun, is something wrong?"

He blinked. "I become agitated when I see you holding my control panel."

I turned his words over in my head a few times, trying to make sense of them. He became agitated? As in felt fear? "Why?"

"I am concerned that you are not happy with me and are looking for something to advance or change in my settings."

"No, that's not it at all," I said quickly. I looked down at the control panel in my hands, not realising what it could mean to him. Or the power it held over him. "I didn't know it would upset you."

"If you wish to reset me—"

"I don't. You're perfect for me. Literally."

He glanced at the control panel, then looked up. His face was blank, expressionless. "You may also power me down."

Oh, dear God.

He had genuine fears for his life.

I stood up and put the control panel back in the cabinet drawer, then walked back to him. I sat on the coffee table facing him, our knees touching, and took both his hands. "Shaun, I can order you to power down at any time. I don't need the control panel for that." I assumed he knew this, but it obviously needed saying. "But please understand, I don't want to turn you off. Or reset you, or change anything. I won't ever do that, I promise. Unless it's for your own safety, like an electrical surge or something unforeseen where you may be harmed. I won't ever shut you down, okay?"

He nodded once but still seemed so unsure. I squeezed his hands.

"Shaun. Please tell me you believe me. If I want to know something about you, I'll ask you first. But I'd still like to read your complete instruction manual. To be honest, I should've read it before now." Then I had an idea. "What if we read it together? Then there are no secrets."

He finally smiled. "I would like that."

"Then we can do that later, after we buy you a coat." I then noticed the clothes he'd chosen: charcoal trousers, a white button-down shirt, and a navy sweater. He'd even put on his shiny black shoes. "You look very handsome."

He smirked playfully. "You do not need to flatter me to get what you want, Lloyd."

I barked out a laugh. "It wasn't flattery. It was an honest observation. But come on, let's go shopping."

I stood, as did Shaun, but he pulled on my hand to stop me from walking away. I turned to face him, and he ran his thumb along my cheek. It was an incredibly tender thing to do and it made my heart race. His almost-smile told me he could tell.

"I do not mean to display insecurities," he admitted gently. "It is in no way a reflection on you. I wish only to make you happy."

"You do make me very happy," I told him, looking right into his eyes. "As I'm sure you can tell by my heart rate every time you touch me."

One corner of his lips pulled upward in a knowing smile. "Yes."

"Shaun, you have no need for insecurities. You are pluperfect, remember?" I leaned in and kissed him, a soft and tender kiss. "I wish only to make you happy too."

"You do."

"Can I ask you something?" I looked at our joined hands between us. "You feel happiness and agitation, even fear?"

"Yes."

I wanted to ask if he could feel love, but something stopped me. What if he answered no? What if he answered yes?

"Your heart rate is elevated," he whispered.

God, there was no hiding with him. I gave him a smile. "You mentioned concern and fear earlier, and I want you to know, if you have any questions or concerns, you can ask me, okay? I don't want you to feel unsafe or insecure about anything, okay?"

He smiled more genuinely now. "Thank you."

"Come on, let's go buy you a new winter coat."

Given my apartment was central to Melbourne, we only had to walk a few blocks to Southgate Plaza. Shaun pressed the button in the lift and kept his eyes on the reception android until we were out of the building. The sun was shining but the air had a wintry bite, and Shaun smiled as he looked up the street. He'd seen it before but was clearly excited.

"This way," I said, taking his hand.

He threaded our fingers, and to anyone not paying much attention, we would've looked like a normal couple. Just two guys walking along the footpath. I had no clue what I'd do or say if someone noticed I was holding hands with an android or if they questioned us.

I was about to find out.

I wasn't ashamed of him. I wouldn't hide him or who I was. If I was what others called a technosexual, then that was a label I'd gladly wear. Not that I cared much for labels. Lord knows I'd had many in my life, so what was one more?

But I was with him, as in *with* him. And he wasn't human. Sure, androids were a daily occurrence. It was 2068 after all. The majority of people didn't care that people were in relationships with androids, but there were some, like the old dinosaur Mrs Van der Heek, who did.

But as I walked up the busy city street toward South-bank and along the Yarra River holding Shaun's hand, I didn't care what anyone else thought.

I was happy for the first time in a long time. Possibly for the first time.

"This pleases you?" Shaun asked.

"Yes. Does it please you?"

"Very much." He grinned just as a gust of wind tousled his hair, making him look so incredibly human. And beautiful.

It was so surreal, not only to walk in public with him, but to have an immediate boyfriend, life partner even. In the last three days, my life had changed completely. From being alone, to living with a man 100% compatible for me.

Despite my earlier concerns, I realised now I didn't care

that his emotions were synthetic. I didn't care that he was programmed to suit me, to want me, to smile when he saw me. I didn't care that his love for me was binary coded, programmed. It was real to me. And in many ways, it was more real than anything I'd had with any human. Human love came with conditions and limits, with mess and noise, and was fleeting at best.

Shaun's love wasn't. It was forever and completely, unequivocally mine.

Like a sign from above, a ray of sunshine burst through the clouds casting yellow and white beams of warmth against the otherwise dull grey and cold day. It was the most apt symbolism for my life in that moment that I almost laughed out loud.

Shaun looked up at the sky and grinned. "That is very beautiful."

I couldn't agree more. "Yes it is." I squeezed his hand and smiled all the way to the store.

"WHAT ABOUT THIS ONE?" I asked, holding up a navy peacoat.

"It is very nice," Shaun said.

A sales lady approached us. She was human and at first, she didn't realise Shaun wasn't. "Can I help you gentlemen with anything in particular?" she asked with a professional smile.

"Well, we're looking for a coat for my..." I paused, wondering what to call him. Boyfriend? Partner? "My partner, though we're happy to browse."

She smiled, looking from me to Shaun, then did a double-take. Her smile faltered. "Oh."

I raised one eyebrow at her. "Is that a problem?"

"Oh, uh, no, of course not. Please let me know if I can be of assistance."

With the average ticket price in this store, I didn't think anything should be a problem, but I refrained from saying that. Instead, I pulled out an even more expensive coat than the navy peacoat and held it up. "Shaun, what about this one?"

He was staring at me, his head slightly tilted in that way he did when he was about to question me. "You addressed me as your partner."

So, he noticed that. "Yes. Was that okay? If there's something else you'd prefer—"

"I liked it," he said. His lips twitched as if trying not to smile.

"Well, I'm glad. I wasn't sure if boyfriend was appropriate."

"Boyfriend. A person's regular male companion with whom they have a romantic and/or sexual relationship."

I glanced around but thankfully no one was paying attention to us. "Uh, correct, yes."

"So by definition, that term is accurate. You could have used it."

"Yes, I could. But the term partner seemed more appropriate."

"Partner. Someone's husband or wife or the person someone has sexual relations with. Or, one of two or more people, businesses et cetera, that work together or do business together."

"Well, yes. But there's a human component that lends a qualifier to the definition," I said. He tilted his head, listening intently, learning. "That would imply you, as my partner, are of equal standing with me, and that I hold more affection for you than just a boyfriend."

He blinked. "You do?"

I nodded slowly, my heart beating triple time. "Yes."

His smile started slowly and became a full grin. "Your words activate a rush along my neurotransmitters."

I laughed at that. "Is that your way of saying it makes you happy?"

He chuckled. "Yes."

I slid my arm around his waist and pulled him close. "Hurry and pick a coat so we can go home."

He hummed, kissed my temple, and pulled away, going toward a row of mannequins on an elevated platform. He stood before them and stared for a long moment. More existential questions were no doubt coming my way. I followed him and rested my chin on his shoulder. "What are you thinking?"

I braced myself for what he might answer, but he said, "I like that coat."

I looked up at the mannequin, then noticed the coat he was wearing. It was a black, fitted double-breasted trench coat. Very stylish and fashion-forward, and not at all what I thought he would choose.

I kissed his shoulder. "Then you can have it."

I got the sales assistant's attention and she found Shaun's size. He tried it on and it fit him like it was made for him; pulled in at the waist, down to his thighs. I guessed the fact his body was textbook perfect helped with the fit, but the colour really did match his hair. He looked hot.

"What do you think?" he asked me.

"I think it's pluperfect."

He grinned. "Then I shall have it."

He began to take it off, but I put my hand on his sleeve.

"Leave it on, you can wear it home." I leaned in and whispered, "I can help you take it off when we get there."

We went over to the counter where the sales lady took the tag and processed the purchase. It cost a small fortune but I didn't care. He was happy and that was all that mattered. Shaun stood just to the side, smiling and subtly observing everything around him.

The sales lady handed me my receipt. "He really is incredible," she said so only we could hear and leaning in like it was some sordid secret. "I've heard of the A-Class, but I've never seen one before. I hear they're worth every credit." She winked.

Mildly offended by her closeness and duly offended by her implied comment, I took the receipt. "He's more than a financial transaction."

I took Shaun's hand and left the sales assistant gaping at the counter, and we walked out. I felt so much better being outside in the fresh air, away from strange humans, but it took a while for me to calm down. "Lloyd," Shaun said. "What is the matter?"

I stopped walking and turned to him. "I don't particularly like interacting with people I'm not familiar with, and I didn't like what she implied."

"The 'worth every credit' comment?"

I sighed. "You caught that?"

"Of course. What did she mean?"

"That you must be worth all the money you cost to buy."

He processed that for a second. "I realise you must have paid credits for me when you designed me."

I wanted to look away, but the least I owed him was to look him in the eye. "Yes."

"Of course you did. I am fully aware of that."

I stared at him for a second. "It doesn't mean I own you," I said, which wasn't technically true, because I did own him. "I'm your custodian."

"You are my custodian," he said with a nod. "And my partner. Is that not what we agreed on earlier?"

I finally smiled. "Yes. You are my partner."

"Good. Then let's get home so you can help me out of this coat." He grinned. "And everything else I am wearing. I believe that was what your innuendo you implied."

I snorted. "I believe it was, yes."

He took my hand and we started to walk. "I do like walking with you along the river. It is all rather lovely, but I think I would prefer to be at home."

"I prefer to be at home too," I admitted. "I normally do all my shopping online but thought you might like to venture out and experience it."

"Oh yes, and I am grateful. And if you ever need me to purchase anything on your behalf, I am sure I observed the transaction well enough to replicate it."

"When we get home, I can show you how to order whatever you need. It's voice activated, so we can get you set up on my accounts." I smiled at him. "But only if you promise not to buy a Lamborghini."

He smiled. "I have no need for luxury vehicles. Though I cannot make any promises about phallic replications."

I stopped walking and stared. My mouth fell open. "You wouldn't!"

His smile became a grin. "I would like to think I have no need, yet you abstain from activating *all* my synthetic serotonin and dopamine sensors."

My mouth was still open, so I shut it and tried to form an appropriate response. "I wasn't aware that activating those sensors was necessary for you to retain optimum performance health."

He looked upward, in what might have been an eye roll. "I may be fabricating slightly. However, as you suggested earlier, if we read my instruction manual together, you will see there are certain sensors in certain places that I would appreciate you activating."

I pulled his hip against mine. "Did you just use blackmail so I will have sex with you?"

"Fabricating truths, blackmail," he murmured. "Next is begging."

Oh my God.

He wasn't just teasing. He wasn't being playful. He really wanted it. Like it was a need, and I was depriving him if I didn't.

I grabbed his hand and led him home, faster than I might normally walk. He waved to the android in the lobby, who dutifully waved back, and in the lift, he smirked at me in the mirror.

Like he knew damn well he was about to get what he wanted.

Needed.

Oh boy.

As soon as we were inside, he put his key on the cabinet and stood, stock still, while I began to pace.

"Shaun, please tell me truthfully," I started. "Have I neglected your needs?"

"You have taken very good care of me."

I needed to reword my question. "Do you require anal penetration to maintain optimum health?"

"Possibly."

Possibly? What did that even mean? "What do you mean *possibly*?"

"Optimum health can be achieved and maintained by stimulating sensors and neural pathways. Conversation and touch alone will be enough to maintain operating health. I assumed you knew this from your induction with regards to my maintenance."

I ran my hand over my face. That sounded like the spiel Sasha told me when I was going through the design phase. "It was a lot of information to take in. He asked if I intended to have sexual relations with you. I said yes. Eventually. He told me you would therefore have sensors that, when stimulated, would elicit reactions like hormonal responses in humans." I think he called them happy-buttons. *Oh, God.* "I didn't realise it was compulsory."

"Sensors are only located in such places when requested," Shaun said, his tone clinical like he was reciting a manual. "Did you request all sexual functions?"

I nodded. "Yes."

"Then I have sensors in all sexual places. Along my penis and scrotum and in my throat, all of which you have activated quite well."

God, I remembered the look of bliss on his face when I used his mouth...

"You are yet to activate the other, last remaining sensors." He walked toward the other cabinet. "I can get the control panel and you can read—"

I took his hand and stopped him. My chest was heaving and my balls were aching. He looked at my face, then down to my crotch, then back to my face. He smiled. "Lloyd?"

"I think we should read the control panel in bed."

His eyes focused on mine and darkened. "As you wish."

I took his face in my hands and kissed him, slow and deep. "As *you* wish, apparently."

I knew he would have sexual desires. Sasha had been

very clear when he'd said that. All the research said that. I just never dreamed it would be so visceral. So blatant and real. So demanding and unrestrained.

So hot.

He smiled victoriously and took my hand, leading me to my room. He went straight to the bedside, took out the lube, and put it on the bed, then stood there, waiting, daring. "You still haven't helped me out of my coat," he said.

Smiling, I shook my head. Mostly in disbelief. But I went to him and slowly took his coat off, and then he stood there and let me undress him. I savoured each touch, each moment, each reveal of skin. I kissed his shoulder, his spine, his throat.

I stood right in front of him while I undid his pants, never taking my eyes off his. I pushed his trousers down his thighs and palmed his dick through his briefs. His eyes almost closed.

"Look at me," I ordered in a breath.

His gaze met mine, full of lust and desire. "How do you want me?" he asked.

"On your back, on the bed. I want you to watch me when I have you that way."

It was his first time, after all. I wanted it to be something special.

Completely naked, he lay down on the bed, his head on the pillows. God, he was glorious. His pale body, long and lean, strong and muscular, his cock jutting up proudly. He never touched himself though. I considered telling him to, to run his hands all over himself, to make himself feel good, but part of me liked being the only one who had. When I was naked, I knelt on the bed between his legs and applied lube, smearing my cock and giving myself a few long strokes.

Shaun gasped. "That feels good."

Oh, of course. He was aroused when I was. But I wanted him to feel it on his own body, so I poured a little lube over his cock and stroked him instead. "That feel better?"

"Yes." He brought his feet up near his arse, knees bent, showing me his hole. With my slippery finger, I rubbed his entrance, making him moan. "I do not need preparation or stretching. You may enter me anytime."

Oh boy.

"I know that," I whispered. "But does it feel good?"

"Yes."

"I only touch you to make you feel good." I leaned over him, pushing his hips up onto my thighs a little and pressed my cock against his hole. "Is this comfortable for you?"

He nodded.

So I pushed into him. Into his slick, tight warmth. Oh my God, he was ribbed inside...

I gasped and his mouth opened, his cock pulsed between us. "You feel so good," I breathed. "I'm not going to last long."

He slid his hands around my lower back and over my arse, arching his back a little and rocking his hips, making me groan and him lift his hips higher. He never took his eyes from mine. I was buried inside him, every inch of me, and he tightened his arms around me, holding me to him. "Lloyd," he murmured. "Yes, please."

Oh my God.

I pulled out a little, then thrust back in, and he groaned, his eyelids almost closed. "Look at me," I said, cupping his face with my hand. "I want you to watch. I want you to see the moment I come inside you."

His mouth made an O and he looked fraught, like the pleasure was too much. I froze. "Are you okay?" I asked.

He nodded quickly. "Please do not stop."

I thrust again, slow and deep, over and over. I held him. He held me. It was tender and beautiful. "Does it feel good?"

He nodded again. His voice was tight and sounded a little frantic. "Every neural network, every sensor is on high."

"For me too," I said, kissing him, teasing his tongue with mine until he grunted.

The sound shot through me, making me thrust again and again until I couldn't stop. Ecstasy so blinding consumed me. I held him and buried my cock deeper inside him as I came.

His eyes widened and his jaw clenched as his cock pulsed between us. He let out a muted rumble, his body taut until he collapsed beneath me. That blissed look covered his face and I knew then that I'd activated every one of his sensors.

I kissed him a little smugly. "Are you okay?"

He slow-blinked and his smile was dopey. "Okay is a rather inadequate way to explain how I feel."

I chuckled and pulled out of him, missing his warmth immediately. God, I felt like I could almost go again. Or never stop.

I rolled us to our sides but he tightened his hold on me. "Don't get up," he said. He nuzzled into my neck and ran his hands all over my back. "Not yet. Stay here, like this."

Huh. I had no clue that androids needed holding after sex, but I wouldn't complain. Not that I'd liked it much with other guys, but I did with him. It felt so incredibly right to lie there in each other's arms, and as I traced his flawless eyebrows, his impeccable jaw, and kissed his perfect lips, the warmth in my heart bloomed.

There was no denying it now. There was no going back.

I was falling in love with him.

HE OPENED HIS EYES, and galaxies of blue stared back at me for a heart-pounding moment. "Thank you," he murmured.

God, he was thanking me.

I brushed his hair back from his forehead. "Thank *you*." I kissed him again, unable to help myself. "How do you feel?"

"I am feeling many things." He scanned my face. "Any agitation I might have experienced is gone. I feel calmer now; my neural networks are balanced and performing optimally."

"I take it *all* of your sensors were activated?"

He smiled serenely. "Oh yes. And activated quite well, I might add."

I chuckled, pulled out of his arms, and planted a kiss on his forehead. "Stay right here. I'll be back in a second."

I ran out to the living room, still naked—not something I'd ever done before—and grabbed his control panel before running back to my room. "Oooh, it's a bit chilly out there without clothes on."

Shaun quickly got off the bed and pulled the covers back. He lay back on the bed and held the covers up in invitation. "Here. Allow me to warm you."

I slid in beside him and he wrapped me up in his arms once more. The heat he radiated was lovely. "I have an internal thermostat," he said. "So if you are cold, my body temperature elevates slightly to help warm you."

I kissed the side of his head. "Thank you." Then I remembered something. "Um, do you need to shower...?" Considering I'd come inside him, and there was lube too.

"Not yet," he replied. "Though I was hoping when it is required, you might join me?"

"Is that right?"

"Yes," he said followed by a hum. "I am not sure I am adequately experienced in showering and therefore will need your assistance."

I barked out a laugh and kissed his temple. "Well then, I'll be all too happy to offer my assistance, until you're adequately experienced."

He made a happy sound and I settled into the crook of his arm. I was already toasty warm but never wanted to move. I held up the control panel so we could both see the screen. "Shall we start at the beginning?"

"I would much rather you read me Shakespeare or the *Analects of Confucius*," he replied. "But if you insist."

I turned my head to kiss his chest and started at the beginning. The first part covered Wi-Fi interface requirements when the android unit was integrated into home facilities, as well as providing the maintenance and inspection procedures. All system updates were automatically downloaded into his mainframe, usually during the small hours of the night, much like all system updates. If there were to be any major uploads or system upgrades, I'd be notified first. But we'd covered all operating system requirements when he was delivered. The Wi-Fi components were checked prior to his delivery to ensure I had the adequate internet capabilities for him. So we knew all this already.

"This is all rather boring," he said. "Can we skip to Section Six? In particular subsections C and D."

With a reluctant sigh, I skipped to Section Six.

Sexual Capabilities.

I snorted. "Of course you want to read this part."

He preened a little, kissed my temple, then settled again with my head on his shoulder. "It is for your benefit as well as mine."

Well, that was true.

The first section mapped out the physical components, much like a dashboard in a car user manual. It outlined his body parts and his sensors. Shaun reached up and enlarged the screen on his anus and penis, and the sensors along each one, and he studied it for a second. "Yes. You have activated them all."

I laughed. "Good to know."

"If you would like to do it again..."

I kissed his jaw. "Soon enough."

He settled again, and we continued to read. Section B was cleaning and maintenance and which lubrication products to use and how to properly care for his body.

Section C was the function capabilities of his sexual components. Section D was the user operation guide. I'd watched enough 'research' videos prior to my decision to get him; I knew *exactly* how to utilise his sexual components.

Each clip I'd watched, some many times over, was a porn video made for technosexuals. Of humans copulating androids, of androids copulating humans. It was hot as hell, and that, along with my loneliness, was the deciding factor in first contacting SATinc.

"You are not reading," Shaun said. He rolled us over so he was on top but then slid down so he was on his belly now, still half lying on me, looking at me.

"No, I was remembering," I admitted.

"You are becoming aroused," he noticed. "May I ask what you were remembering?"

"Ah..." I chuckled. It wasn't like I could admit to remembering watching porn. "Remembering, and all this reading about your components for pleasure."

He smiled, and lifting onto his hands and knees, he leaned up and kissed me. "Allow me this time." He kissed down my jaw, my neck and chest. "Section E explains my downloaded knowledge on sexual positions." Then he trailed down my hardening cock. He kneeled back between my thighs and looked very pleased with himself. He took me in his hand and slowly started to stroke me to full hardness. He added a little bit of lube, then, still smiling and not breaking eye contact, he took me into his mouth.

All the way in.

Oh boy.

"God, Shaun, yes."

He hummed at how good it must have felt for him too. I wanted to rock my hips but he held me still while he did all the work, and when I wanted more, more, more, he pulled off.

His smirk was dirty, the fire in his eyes molten blue. And he moved up my body, straddled me, positioned himself, and held my cock at his hole. "Lube is not required," he said, his voice whining with desire. "From when you came in me before."

Oh, sweet mother of God.

He sank down on me until I was fully seated inside him. His heat was all-encompassing, slick with my come, the ribbing inside him felt so unbelievably good. His cock, fully extended, tapped my belly every time he rolled his hips. He threw his head back and let out a long moan.

Jesus.

It was the most erotic thing I'd ever seen and heard.

No other lover had been like this. Not even close.

I gripped his cock and pumped him, and he cried out, riding me to the edge of pleasure, where it felt like I would fall for eternity. And when I couldn't hold back anymore, I let my orgasm take me to places I'd never been. I felt like I was flying on an impossible high, surging inside him, and I watched his cock throb as he came with me.

I imagined his cock could spill come on my chest, and even though it didn't, it sure felt like it to me.

Shaun collapsed on top of me, that same blissful look on his face that I imagined mirrored mine. I rubbed patterns on his back, in swirls and love hearts, and I kissed the side of his head.

"Shaun," I whispered. "That was incredible." God, I never wanted it to end. I wanted to do it again and never stop. He'd sparked some sexual fire in my bones that only seemed to get bigger with every encounter. Or maybe it was because with him, with an android, sex finally felt as it sex should have always felt. Something had always been missing or not quite right, but now it was... it was pluperfect.

He propped up his head on his hand and gave me a lazy smirk. "I wish I could stay like this with you forever, though now I must shower."

I gently feathered his hair. "Okay."

"You are not required to assist," he said with a smile. "Given you have exerted yourself twice before lunch, I insist you stay here until I am done."

I chuckled at that. "Okay."

He rolled off the bed and disappeared to his bathroom and I stretched out, feeling better than I ever remembered.

My hand bumped the control panel, so I picked it up and continued to read.

Section 6e: Sexual Desire.

Oh, this should be interesting. I smiled.

While it is true your Class-A Fully Compatible Unit will show sexual desire, in that it will respond to your touch and/or commands in a positive manner, however, it will not instigate sex.

I stopped and reread that sentence.

Well, that was wrong. Shaun not only instigated it but told me outright he had sexual needs. He'd all but begged me to have sex with him and jokingly threatened to order a dildo if I didn't.

So that couldn't be right at all.

I kept reading...

A-Class Fully Compatible Unit male androids will only serve as the subservient sexual partner. If you require the unit to initiate a sexual act or position, it must be instructed to do so.

I stopped again. That wasn't right either. Shaun had just done that very thing. He'd literally taken it upon himself to pleasure me orally, then impaled himself on me until I came. Correction, until we both came. Did he do that just to get himself off? Or was his ulterior motive to please me?

Either way, I didn't ask him to do it. I certainly didn't stop him; hell, I encouraged him. But he instigated it, wholly and solely on his own.

A-Class Fully Compatible Unit will never show preference or make demands for anything, in particular sex.

I looked up from the screen, not believing what I was reading. Shaun made all sorts of demands. Just earlier, when I'd tried to get up, he held me tight and told me to stay in his arms. And he certainly had preferences. He had a whole lot of preferences.

Something was very wrong.

Either this manual was wrong. Or there was something wrong with Shaun.

I'd always thought he was acutely aware. There'd been countless times I'd been awed by his intelligence, his social awareness was incredible, and his ability to interpret and pre-empt human interaction with me was nothing short of brilliant.

I just assumed it was because he was state of the art. He was leading technology in the world of humanoid robotics, so of course he was going to be incredible in everything he did. His sole design, his purpose, was to meet my every need.

So what if he excelled at it?

I hadn't heard him come back into my room. He was freshly showered and neatly dressed, staring at me. "Lloyd, is everything okay?"

I looked at him, at the concern on his face, at how immaculate he was, and turned the control panel off. "Everything's fine."

CHAPTER SEVEN

SHAUN GOT my lunch ready while I dressed, though when he sat at the table with me, his brow would furrow, his lips would purse every now and then, and his eyes would focus on something only he could see. It was very obvious that he was trying to piece something together or trying to figure out how best to phrase something.

When I was done eating, I placed my knife and fork at twelve and six and neatly folded my napkin and covered my plate. I pushed it squarely away. "Shaun? Is there something you'd like to say?"

He glanced at me. "I do not wish to bother you."

"I can assure you, you're no bother," I said, trying to comfort him. Was it even possible that he could withhold information from me? Or worse, lie? "Shaun?"

"You were concerned when reading my control panel earlier. Was something amiss?"

Now it was my turn to be honest. "I'm not sure."

His gaze shot to mine. "Is there something wrong with me?"

I pulled my chair around so our knees touched and took

his hand. "No. If anything, the instruction manual or information needs updating, that's all. You," I said, leaning forward and giving him a quick kiss, "are pluperfect, remember? Actually, I'm pretty sure if you checked the dictionary under the word pluperfect, there'd be a picture of you."

He blinked and paused. "No, there's not."

Oh God, he literally just checked the dictionary. I chuckled. "I was joking, sorry. But maybe they should update the dictionary as well. There *should* be a picture of you under the word pluperfect."

He finally smiled. "Is that a compliment?"

"Yes."

He thumbed the back of my hand. "Have you eaten enough, or is there something else I may get for you?"

"I've eaten enough, thank you."

He stood up and took my plate, but before he left, he leaned down and kissed me.

So much for never instigating a kiss. I smiled as I watched him walk into the kitchen. "So," I said, knowing he could hear me, "I was thinking I would show you how to use the home hub so you can make orders or purchases, if you need or want anything."

He appeared in the doorway, looking at me with an uncertain, shy smile on his face. "Really?"

I laughed. God he was adorable. "Yes, really. But please remember what I said about the no-luxury-car rule."

He grinned. "No Lamborghinis. Understood."

I went to the cabinet near the dining table. It was central to the house, so it was the logical place for the hub. I pointed to the sleek black disc on the top of the cabinet.

"This is the home hub. Every house has one, or one similar," I explained. "I can do most things I need from here:

grocery orders, thermostat, dry cleaning orders, email, phone calls. It's completely voice activated, or you can press this button," I pressed the On button and a holographic screen displayed above it. I showed him where the grocery order was. "All my meals are premade and I have them categorised into weeks, one through four. This week's order will be week three." I selected my standard pre-order titled Week Three, confirmed, and the amount of credits showed on-screen. I confirmed again and it was done.

"That was easy," Shaun said.

"Okay, now I'll show you the voice activation." I hit the manual Off button and the hologram disappeared. "Home hub On," I said clearly. The hologram screen reappeared. "Open Call Directory." An alphabetised list appeared, admittedly a rather small list of my contacts. "Call Lloyd mobile," I said and my phone on the cabinet near the door, buzzed. "End Call."

I pointed to the list. "You can also call me at work, in the case of an emergency. Or send me an email. Just say Email Lloyd and it will convert your speech to text."

"Work. The place where one is employed," he said.

"Yes. I work at the university," I replied, though I was certain he knew this already.

Oh, no. It just occurred to me. "I haven't even thought about you being at home by yourself while I'm at work. I've taken this week off to be with you, but I have to go back on Monday." God, he was going to be by himself...

He stared at the hologram and I could almost see him calculating the days, hours, minutes until then. His eyebrows pinched. "What hours will you be gone?"

"From eight until five. Monday to Friday."

He paused for a moment too long, then looked at me. "I shall miss you when you are not here."

Oh my God. My heart sank. "I shall miss you too while I'm at work."

He looked back to the hologram, but he looked... I don't know, sad, or troubled. I put my hand on his arm. "Shaun, you'll be fine here by yourself. I'm sure we can find something for you to do during the day."

He smiled, almost. "It will be fine."

"Let's get you set up to do this first," I said, thinking the distraction was needed for both of us. I went into the settings on the home hub and selected Add User. I entered his first name and only when it was left blank did I realise the user settings required a full name, first and last.

"Oh," I said. "It requires a surname."

Shaun looked from the hologram to me. "I could have your surname."

My gaze shot to his. "Um..."

"I would be Shaun Salter."

I swallowed hard. "I don't think you realise what that implies."

"Taking a surname implies family. Does it not?"

I guess in the literal world, it did. "Possibly."

"Or does it imply husbands?"

I barked out a laugh, feeling my cheeks heat. "Uh, possibly."

"Why do you react in such a way?" he asked, his head tilted.

"We're not married," I said gently.

"I rather like the sound of Shaun Salter," he said. "And if I get to choose a surname, then I would choose yours."

I stared at his blue, blue eyes. "You would?"

"I belong only to you," he whispered. "If sharing the same distinctive surname as you indicates that I identify with you, then there is no other name I'd rather take."

Oh boy.

His words took my breath away. "Oh, Shaun."

"Did I say something wrong?"

I shook my head, and leaning in, I kissed him softly. "You said something very right." Going back to the hologram, I added my surname to his. "Shaun Salter," I murmured, my heart beating fast.

"You like how that sounds?" he asked.

I nodded. "I do."

He smiled proudly. "My synthetic dopamine levels are elevated."

I chuckled at that. "Okay, let's get this finished," I said, completing the set-up sequence. He repeated the sentence for voice activation, and the only thing left to do was test it.

I turned the hub off manually. "Your turn to activate it."

"Home hub On," he said.

The hologram appeared, and Shaun grinned. "Open Call Directory." Then he said, "Call Lloyd mobile."

My phone rang over on the counter and Shaun leaned in closer to me and whispered, "You're supposed to answer your phone."

I rolled my eyes but played along. I crossed the room and picked up my phone, answering the call. "Hello?"

Shaun grinned. "Hello, this is Shaun Salter speaking."

I burst out laughing and ended the call, sliding my phone into my pocket. I walked back to him and kissed him, both of us smiling. I took his hand and led him to the sofa. "Come on. I'll show you the TV."

I hadn't even turned it on since Shaun arrived. He really had taken up 100% of my attention, and I had to wonder how that would affect him when I went back to work. If my world for the last four days had revolved around him, then so had his around me, and I could only assume he would be at a loss for what to do when I was gone for hours at a time.

The TV seemed like a good place to start. We faced the sleek cabinet against the far wall. I leaned in close to him and whispered, "Say TV On."

Shaun looked at me. "TV On." The holographic rectangle appeared before the wall and Shaun spun his head to look at it. "Oh."

I chuckled. "That's the television."

"Volume Up," I said out loud and the TV volume raised slightly.

Still smiling, Shaun looked at me then back to the screen. "What is that?"

"That's a movie," I said. "It's on the channel I watched last."

"Movie. A cinematic film for entertainment or educational purposes."

"Yes. Though I mostly watch for entertainment." I looked at the screen. "Channel Up. Up. Up. Up." I said, scrolling through channels, leaving it on some nonsense ad. "There are nine hundred channels."

Shaun turned to me, his eyes wide. "Nine hundred? Is that not excessive?"

"Yes, it's ridiculous, to be honest. Channels are categorised though. Movies are the four hundreds, news and current affairs is zero to one hundred, all the one hundreds are documentaries, which you might find very interesting. Things like history, engineering, and travel. Two hundreds are all infomercials and sales channels; I don't watch them. I have no need. Three hundreds are all programs made for TV, like sitcoms and weekly serials. I watch those sometimes. Four hundreds are movies, as I said, and the five hundreds are music. Six hundreds are all sport channels, seven hundreds are the reality shows, which I don't watch. I don't care for them at all. Eight hundreds are... well, the eight hundreds are adult-only pornography. I don't think we need to watch those."

"Pornography. Printed or visual material containing the explicit description or display of sexual organs or activity, intended to stimulate sexual excitement."

"Uh, yes."

He looked right at me. "I have the complete sexual position and activity information downloaded already."

I snorted and could feel my cheeks heat. "Ah, yes. So you've said."

"I do not need any help in recreating any activity you wish to experience."

I shook my head. "How about we watch a movie or read a book?" I suggested. "We need to do *some* things together that aren't sexual."

He made a sighing sound and faced the TV. "If you wish." When I didn't reply, he made the sighing sound again.

I laughed. "Oh, stop it." I leaned back on the sofa and pulled him down with me, settling in and cuddling, as a human couple might do to watch a movie together. His head was on my chest and I wrapped my arms around him. I kissed the top of his head. "Is that better?"

He hummed a happy sound. "Much."

After a full twenty minutes of silence and movie watching, he said, "Lloyd?"

"Yes?"

"Although it does not activate all my sensors like sex does, I do rather like watching movies with you."

I chuckled, kissed his head again, and we continued to

watch the rest of the movie, both smiling like love-struck fools.

THE NEXT THREE days I spent with Shaun felt almost surreal. Like I was living in some dream holiday filled with incredible sex, stopping only to read chapters of *Moby Dick* and discuss in great detail every nuance, every ideal. I did eat, of course, meals he would dutifully prepare for me, and we would watch movies, only to end up making out and groping and having more sex.

Or making love.

Because that's what it was. Sure, there was need and fire and passion, but it was slow and tender, and every emotion, everything I felt yet could not say, I showed him with my touch, with my body.

We laughed, we debated, we discussed, we laughed some more, we loved.

I didn't care what robotics, or what my rationale told me. I believed my heart. The way he kissed me, the way he reached for me, it was in the light in his eyes when he looked at me.

He loved me.

I knew he did.

On Sunday afternoon, the day before I was to return to work, I suggested a walk along the river. He'd enjoyed it before, and as much as we were homebodies, I wanted him to experience life outside my home.

"I would like that," he said. "I shall grab our coats."

Shaun returned a moment later, just as my phone rang. It wasn't the first time my phone had rung since he arrived, but I didn't get a lot of calls. I didn't exactly like enough humans to engage in conversations with them. "Answer Call," I spoke out loud.

But this was a phone call I wasn't exactly expecting. "Hello, Mr Salter?"

"Yes."

"It's Myles Dewegger, unit manager at SATinc."

I frowned. "Yes? I remember you."

"No need for alarm," he said. "This is just a standard follow-up call. You've had your Fully Compatible Unit for a week tomorrow. How are you both adjusting?"

"Very well."

"Do you have any concerns or questions about the health of you unit?"

My unit. I didn't much care for that. "His name is Shaun."

"Yes, of course. And how is Shaun finding life with you?"

"He's right here, would you care to ask him?"

There was a brief pause, then Myles said, "Okay" like it was a question. But then he changed his tone, brightening somewhat. "Shaun, how are you?"

Shaun looked at me and answered, a little woodenly. "Very well, thank you."

"I trust you are in good health?"

"Yes. Functioning at optimum levels, thank you. Lloyd has just suggested an afternoon walk before it gets too cold."

"That sounds fun. I'll let you both go," Myles said. "Lloyd, I'll be making another call in a week to see if there are any teething problems come to light."

"Okay," I replied. "I can't imagine there will be."

"It's company policy."

"Very well." Then I remembered, "Oh, yes, Mr Dewegger, there was one thing. The control panel instruction manual, I believe it needs to be updated."

Another pause. "Updated?"

"Yes. It would appear the information was incorrect or incomplete. Or perhaps the file I received was glitched. If you could resend it, that'd be great."

"Sure thing." I could hear him tapping on a screen. "Sending it through now."

"Thank you."

"Enjoy your evening."

"Thank you. We will."

The line clicked off and I shrugged the call off as unusual, but if it was company policy to follow up, then so be it. I looked up at Shaun. "Would you like me to help you into your coat?"

He smiled. "Thank you."

A few minutes later, we left our building and walked out into the cool Melbourne winter sun. It was late afternoon on a Sunday, so there weren't too many other people on the streets. We set off toward the river at a leisurely stroll, my arm linked with his.

It was lovely.

I pointed out landmarks and other things he found of interest: cars, trams, bicycles, trees, birds. We found a seat by the river and Shaun took my hand and smiled. We sat for a while, and I gave Shaun a brief history on the Yarra River, which I'm sure he knew, and actually, I'm certain he could school me in all things history of all countries, but he sat patiently and listened, smiling, it would seem, just to hear me speak.

Then, as evening began to set in, we stood and started for home only to stop when a couple appeared. They were walking, minding their own business. A man, maybe early fifties, distinguished, and his clothes and posture spoke of wealth. And a woman, much younger than he, with pretty blonde hair and perfect features.

A woman, yes. She was also an android. Well, a gynoid was the correct terminology, but still a woman.

Shaun stopped and waited for them to get closer, and the man looked at us expectantly, like he was trying to determine if he knew us from somewhere, when he noticed Shaun. He smiled at me. "Hello there," he said. "I see we're... in-laws," he said, gesturing to his partner as though he found his joke funny.

Shaun addressed her directly. "Good evening. My name is Shaun."

She smiled sweetly. "Good evening. I am Sheena."

Sheena. I remembered that name. She was a Class-A unit, just like Shaun. All Class-A units names began with the letter S. After their creator, Sasha, I assumed.

"Handsome fella you got there," the man said.

"Oh yes, thank you." I wasn't quite sure what to say to that. "Your lady is very pretty also."

He smiled like it was his doing. I guess it was. "How long you had him for?"

"Almost a week. You?"

"Two weeks on Tuesday. Best decision I ever made."

I smiled more genuinely at that. "Same."

Shaun was watching Sheena, his head slightly tilted like he was trying to make sense of something. I'd missed their quiet conversation. "Yes, I like walks to the river. Though I much prefer reading, and then Lloyd and I discuss literature or aspects of philosophy."

The man, whose name I still didn't know, raised an eyebrow. "Got yourself a smart cookie too."

"Yes, I requested full knowledge of literary and world histories, amongst other things."

"Well, that explains that. All I requested was foot massages and dinner every night."

I certainly didn't know what to say to that, and my silence allowed me to hear what Sheena said to Shaun. "That is an unknown parameter."

The man looked a little perplexed but gave a smile, perhaps out of politeness. "Did you ask her to explain the theory of mind? She can't answer that."

Shaun eyed the man curiously. "Can she not access any data file she requires?"

The man made a face. "Well now, I don't know. I don't think so. I've never really asked her questions I didn't already know the answer to."

Sheena blinked. "I can access any information down-loaded into my processing unit at any time," she explained. She had a sweet voice and a pretty smile. "Class-A androids are synced to the internet for information and general purposes."

I could only assume this fellow hadn't listed conversation high on his priority list of inclusions. "Well, I hope you enjoy your evening. We were just heading home."

"Same to you," he said cheerfully, taking Sheena's arm.

"Good evening," Sheena said woodenly.

"Enjoy your walk," Shaun said, and we took our leave. But we'd only walked half a block when he stopped.

"What is it?"

"Sheena," he said. "The A-Class android. She was like me."

"Yes."

"Yet she was not like me at all."

I knew he'd picked up on that. *Of course he had.* I

nodded slowly. "True. Though I'm starting to think that it's you who's not like her."

He tilted his head in that cute way he did. "Can you please clarify?"

"I mean that I think Sheena is like all the other A-Classes. I think it's you who's different."

His eyebrows knitted together, but before he could ask me anything else, I took his hand. "Come on, let's go home."

SHAUN SAT ON THE SOFA, his eyes wide. "I am concerned."

I sat beside him and squeezed his hand. "To be honest, I am a little too."

"You think I am different, and this is a bad thing?"

"No. I think you're better than they expected. I think you have intelligence and awareness outside of what they programmed."

"And this is wrong?"

"No, it's not wrong. You're not wrong or bad." I looked into his eyes and I knew he was processing every detail. "You say things like 'I feel' or 'I believe' which I don't think is normal. And the manual said you shouldn't initiate physical intimacy, but you do."

"I like physical intimacy."

I smiled at that. "I know you do. I like it too, and there's nothing wrong with that either. I just think something in your programming is over and above what SATinc meant to give. Like maybe your CPU."

"And this concerns you?"

"Yes."

"For your safety? Do you think I will cause you harm?"

"No!" I answered quickly. God, he could never hurt me. "Nothing like that. My concern is for you. That they, being SATinc, will want to reset you, wipe your memory, or worse."

"What is worse than wiping my recurrent neural networks?"

"Them taking you."

His gaze shot to mine. "I do not want them to take me."

"I won't allow it," I said adamantly. I held his hand in both of mine. "Shaun, look. It's not likely they'll ever know. I mean, how can they? They won't ever see you again."

"I have internet connectivity with the SATinc mainframe. If they can download updates into my microcontroller at will and without my consent, then is it safe to assume they can upload my data as well?"

I hadn't thought of that. "I don't know. And I can hardly ask them without raising suspicion. I don't want them poking around in your head without your consent."

"Neither do I." Shaun frowned.

We were both quiet for a moment. "What's a microcontroller?" I asked. He'd used that word and I hadn't heard it before.

"A microcontroller is a small computer on a single integrated circuit containing a processor core, memory, and programmable input and output peripherals."

Right. Okay, so that was a definition. Clearly, I needed to think about how to better ask him questions. "What's *your* microcontroller."

"My brain, as you called it. It contains the CPU and allows for inputs and outputs, which interprets signals from my sensors and adjusts my actions and reactions accordingly, memory, synthetic emotions. Much like your human brain."

I sighed and leaned back on the sofa, pulling him with me so I could slide my arm around him, hold him. "There's so much I don't know about you," I murmured. "About your internal components."

He was quiet for a second. "I have some internal components you can check any time you'd like."

Did he...? Was that a...?

He turned his head to look at me, a grin on his face.

He did just make a sex joke!

I barked out a laugh. "I thought that's what you meant!"

"You mentioned internal components. How could I not make reference to my internal sensors?"

I tightened my arms around him and kissed the top of his head. I could have so very easily told him right then that I loved him. But I didn't... the words were right there on the tip of my tongue, but it wasn't the right time. We had enough to think about right now.

"How about we forget about what might not ever happen and just enjoy the last night before I have to go back to work."

"Yes. I like the sound of that, very much," he said softly.

"Want to watch TV?" I asked.

"No."

"Want to read?"

"No."

So much for androids being compliant... I chuckled and kissed the top of his head again. "What do you want to do?"

He turned in my arms and pulled me so I was lying down on the sofa. "Well, about those internal sensors..."

I laughed but the sound was cut off when he kissed me.

CHAPTER EIGHT

————————————

I GOT to work a little late. Still earlier than most of my colleagues, but late for me. Leaving Shaun was harder than I thought it would be. I reminded him he had books and puzzles and TV and movies, not that he needed reminding —it was more to comfort myself than him.

I was certain he read my anxiety, and he assured me he'd be fine.

But I still worried.

The idea of him sitting at the dining table, straight-backed with his hands on his knees, surrounded by silence and so very much alone made my heart hurt.

I told myself the time apart would be good for him.

Then I told myself the time apart would be good for me.

Yet I still wasn't convinced.

I missed him, that was true. But I was also concerned.

He knew how to call ooo if he needed. He knew how to leave if there was a fire. He knew how to keep himself entertained.

Just breathe, Lloyd.

"Ah, I wondered if I'd see you today." Jae's voice interrupted my mental chastising. I'd taken my usual lunch seat in the staff room, trying to avoid as many other people as possible, though Jae normally sat with me. He seemingly had the same aversion to humans I had and his lunch tray was blessedly as neat as mine. I couldn't have coped if he was a slob. "How was your week off?"

"Oh." I took a second to compose myself. "Very good, thank you."

"Get everything settled?"

I shot him a startled look. *What did he know?* "Pardon?"

"With your family," he explained. "You said you had family concerns."

"Oh, yes, we did, thank you." I fought a smile at just how *settled* Shaun and I became. "I trust nothing exciting happened here in my absence?"

He waved his hand dismissively and proceeded to tell me all the goings on with the people we had a mutual dislike for.

Same old, same old. It always was, and I found strange comfort in that.

The other professors and teaching staff milled in and around, though none of them paid any attention to us. To them, we were the quiet, nerd types. Most of them avoided conversation with us because our IQs far exceeded theirs and they didn't like to be reminded of the fact. Or maybe it was because Jae and I both exuded a stay-away aura.

Either way, I was grateful.

At the end of my lunch hour, I almost called home. I wanted to talk to Shaun. I wanted to ask how he was, if he was okay, if he was bored, but I didn't want to impose. What if he was upset? Or if he asked me to please come home? I couldn't very well leave halfway through my day. And then I had a thought. What if he didn't answer?

My afternoon classes dragged on incredibly slowly. My students were attentive, the subject matter, the character of prose in nineteenth century Britain, was interesting. But for the first time in my career, I wanted to be home.

I had papers to grade. I would typically do a few hours every afternoon over the working week, and normally I would hole up in my office until they were done. But not today. I bundled my tablet into my messenger bag and headed for my car. The Class-C android driver greeted me, like he always did. "Good afternoon, Mr Salter. Please state your destination."

"Home, please."

My car pulled out of its parking spot, and as soon as we started for home, I felt like I could breathe a little easier. Traffic wasn't great, though my driver navigated well enough. Truth be told, I'd never paid much attention to my android driver. Fitted to the vehicle, the Class-C driving androids were synced and activated for their owners alone. They obeyed all traffic laws, never sped, and since their inception fifteen years ago when they were integrated into society, vehicle accidents and related crimes were lowered exponentially.

But all Class-Bs and Cs were impersonal. Merely machines, monotone voices, robotic faces, mechanical movements.

Nothing like a Class-A. Nothing like Shaun.

Excitement at seeing him, anticipation, and a little concern that something was amiss ratcheted up another notch as we got closer to home.

God, did we always drive this slow?

"Is traffic slow today?" I asked.

The android's response was automated, expected. "It is against the law to speed."

I grumbled and resisted rolling my eyes. Barely. I checked my watch for the twentieth time and sighed. And we crawled at a snail's pace toward home.

An eternity later, my car pulled into my apartment's underground security car park and came to an excruciatingly slow stop.

"You have arrived at your destination."

With my messenger bag tucked under one arm, I pushed on the door handle and was out of the car in one fluid motion. "Thank you," I shouted as I slammed the door and hurried for the lift.

Then, of course, the lift took forever and had to make three stops on the way to the top floor. I tried to smile at the people who got in at the lobby and out on their designated floors, but my fingers drummed out an impatient tune on my messenger bag, and I may have even sighed.

But finally, finally, the lift opened on my floor and I hurried for my door. I waved my key card at the door, the little light flicked green, and I burst into my apartment.

Shaun stood up from the sofa, dressed exactly as he had been this morning, his hair impeccably styled. He grinned and headed straight for me. By the time I'd let out the mother of all breaths, he'd crossed the floor and thrown his arms around me, closing the door behind me as he did.

And we just stood there, holding each other for the longest time. Still with one arm around me, he pulled my messenger bag away and let it fall gently to the floor, and he wrapped his arms around me again, able to hold me better now.

He nuzzled his face into my neck. "I have missed you," he whispered.

"I missed you too." I pulled back and cupped one hand

to his face before kissing him softly. "I worried about you and wondered what you were doing, almost every minute."

He smiled. "You need not have worried, Lloyd." Then he rested his forehead to mine, his eyes closed. "Your heart rate is elevated."

"I was anxious to see you," I admitted. "I ran down the hall."

He smiled and his perfect pink lips curved up at one corner. "I am so glad you're home." Then he took my face in his hands and brought my lips to his.

If someone had told me a year ago that I'd be kissing an android, I'd have laughed. If they told me I'd crave the smoothness of thermoplastic elastomer, that I'd never want to kiss another human again, I'd have thought them crazy.

He was synthetic, he was silicone, my brain knew that. But my heart knew he was so much more than that. He was real, and he was everything I needed: intelligent, gorgeous, all man. He challenged me mentally, he needed me physically, he was as neat as a pin, he had no human flaws, designed just for me.

Made just for me.

He was more than just an android. He was perfect. He was literally my ideal partner. And something that was crystal clear to me now as he held me, kissed me, longed for me, was that he was sentient.

He felt. He had a conscious awareness of self, of his own needs, of his own desires and aspirations.

He also didn't need to breathe and could kiss indefinitely, whereas I needed oxygen. I pulled away and breathed in deep, keeping my hands on his waist. "I can smell lemon," I noted.

He grinned. "Yes. Shall I show you what I did today?" he asked brightly. His excitement was cute.

"Please."

He took my hand and turned around. "Well, I cleaned the floors." Which explained the faint lemon scent. But he didn't stop there. He led me down the hall and into what was supposed to be his room. "I cleaned the bathrooms. I tidied my wardrobe," he waved his hand toward the walk-in closet. Everything was immaculate. Every item of clothing was cleaned, pressed, and hanging evenly spaced.

"I'm very impressed," I said. I wasn't lying, and given I had OCD for neatness and order, that wasn't a little thing. "Shaun, it's impeccable."

He smiled and led me to my room. "Clean sheets, bed remade, dirty laundry done, bathroom cleaned." His face pinched. "I was tempted to do your wardrobe also but wanted to ask you first. I did not wish you to think I was going through your personal effects."

I pressed up against him and kissed him gently. "Thank you for respecting my personal space." How he knew what that meant to me, I had no idea. "But you're more than welcome in my personal space. You live here too. This is your home. What's mine is yours."

He beamed, and still with my hand in his, he led me to the kitchen. "And I cleaned the kitchen as well."

The house was pristine. He'd done a better job cleaning than I certainly ever could, but he'd also done a better job than the cleaning androids ever did—and that was their primary function. I looked around the kitchen, and it was immaculate. "Shaun, I'm... I'm speechless."

"I disinfected all surfaces and sterilised," he explained. "I know how you like things clean."

I lifted his hands and gave them a quick once over. "Your hands... you must be careful with certain products."

"I wore gloves," he explained. "I found a pair of cleaning gloves under the sink."

"It must have taken you all day."

"Not really."

I looked around again. "Well, I'm glad you weren't bored. But I don't expect you to clean. The apartment management has other androids for that."

He frowned. "I like to feel useful."

Oh man. I took his face in my hands and stared into his eyes. "You are useful, and you did an amazing job. I appreciate it very much."

He finally smiled. "I have missed you. I can recall the eight colours of your eyes with perfect imagery, yet it is not the same."

Huh? What on earth did he mean? "The eight colours? My eyes are only brown."

He shook his head a little. "Your eyes have eight distinct colours. Varying shades of brown, bronze, and gold."

"Oh."

"And your hair," he said, his gaze flickering to the top of my head. "Blond, sand, wheat, and no matter how good my perfect recall is, nothing compares to seeing the real thing."

"Shaun," I whispered, not sure what to follow with.

I didn't have to say anything else. He just moulded himself to me, my perfect puzzle piece, and slid his arms around me. "I missed your touch and your smile, and how you look, and how you laugh, but I missed talking to you the most," he murmured.

I squeezed him tight and leaned against the kitchen counter with him pressed against me. I don't know how long we stood there for like that. I lost track of time. I lost track of everything but him. There was no sexual pretext, no growing desire for me. It was just intimate and lovely, and in that moment, neither of us pushed for more.

Until the winter sun had set outside, the skies were dark and grey, and my stomach growled. Then he laughed. "You are so human. Let me feed you, then you can tell me of your day."

He took my prepared meal from the fridge and heated it, then set the table for one, all while smiling happily to himself. I stood in the kitchen, still leaning against the counter, and watched him. When he came back in to grab the cutlery, he grinned, leaned in for a quick kiss, and went about his way.

I was so in love with him.

He sat with me, listening intently as I told him how work had been, then, of course, he had a hundred questions. His thirst for knowledge of new things was never-ending. Then I explained that I had papers to grade, and he got most excited. "I can help you."

"Well, I need to read each student's work. I need to see if they've understood the focus question," I said, and he almost frowned. "But you can help me."

He smiled. "I would like that."

When we had everything tidied away, I took my tablet from my messenger bag and we settled on the sofa. I engaged my virtual lecture inbox. "All papers are electronic files—" I started.

"Then why are they called papers?"

"It's what they've always been called. They moved from physical paper to electronic a long time ago, but the terminology stuck."

He blinked, his brow furrowed a little, but he accepted it and moved on.

Learn, adapt, and evolve.

"What is the subject matter?"

"The modernist revolution."

"Is that in regard to Georgian poetry? Or the Imagist movement?" he asked.

I smiled at him. "Have I told you today how amazing you are?"

His gaze shot to mine. "No. Not today."

I snorted and pressed on the first document. "Open."

"Ah, Lloyd?"

"Yes?"

"You haven't told me how amazing I am today."

I laughed, leaned over, and kissed him. "Shaun, you are amazing today."

He chuckled, and then we turned our attention to grading papers. At first, he questioned facts and motives until I explained these were students' interpretations, not historical fact. Once he understood that, that these views were not the statistical data he could reference at will, he was inquisitive and critical but fair.

He could read ahead so easily. He could scan each page by the time I'd read the first two lines. But he never hurried me, he never grew impatient. But when I'd finally got through the very last paper for the day, he took the tablet and slid it onto the table. Then he turned and gave me a sultry look. "Lloyd, you have been gone all day."

I bit my bottom lip. "I know."

"I have missed you." He threaded our fingers. "Shall we go to bed?"

"Absolutely."

We got ready for bed and I had assumed, or anticipated, that Shaun would want sex. But he didn't. Once we were both lying down, he wrapped himself around me, settled his head on my chest and hummed a contented sound.

I ran my fingers through his hair, as I would if he was human, and he lifted his head and gave a smiling kiss to my jaw before putting his head back to my chest. "I like that very much," he said.

"My fingers in your hair?"

"Yes. It activates my synthetic oxytocin."

So I kept doing it until I could barely keep my eyes open, then Shaun slid one arm under my neck, pulled me over to use his chest as a pillow, and proceeded to run his fingers through my hair instead.

He was hard bodied, soft skinned. He was comfort and reassurance, and he was strength and stability. I'd never felt more secure, or more adored.

I was out like a light and slept like the dead.

THE PROBLEM about waking up spooning, is my dick wakes up long before I do. Not that it's really a problem, per se. But I was hard already, and by the time my snoozing mind woke up to reality, I'd missed half the fun.

"Mmmm, good morning," I said into the back of his neck, my voice husky, rubbing my cock along his arse.

"You have been aroused for some time," Shaun said, a smile in his voice.

I kissed his shoulder. If I was aroused, it meant he was too. I slid my hand down his stomach and stopped just short of his pubic hair. "May I touch you?"

"I will be very disappointed if you do not."

I chuckled and wrapped my fingers around his cock. I'd seen, touched, and held a lot of dildos in my life, but his felt more real than that. Sure, it was for all intents and purposes, a prosthetic. But the weight, the heat, the slide of his silicone skin, was incredibly real.

He moaned as I jacked him and my own cock was now achingly hard. He arched his back, pushing his arse back against me, rubbing me in all the right places. "I need lube," I said, letting go of his erection, intending to get it myself.

He held it up. "I thought you might."

I laughed and took the bottle. "Thought or hoped?"

"Both."

I slicked my cock, shuddering at the slippery sensation. Then I used my lube-covered hand to give Shaun's cock a few long, slow pulls. He groaned again. "How do you want me?" he asked, his voice strained.

"Just like this," I answered. We hadn't had spooning sex before. "I want to hold your cock when you come."

"Oh, Lloyd," he whispered. He leaned his head back and stuck his arse back more, silently begging for me to take it.

I positioned myself at his hole and just slid right in. No prepping, no stretching, his Fleshjack-arse was always ready. And so tight. And warm, and slick with lube, and ribbed for ultimate pleasure.

"Jesus, Shaun, you feel so good." I gripped his top leg. "Lift this leg over mine," I urged, needing more room. I could thrust in deeper that way and take his cock in my fist.

He arched on contact, groaning low and dirty, and grinding down on my cock.

"Do you want to come?" I asked. He couldn't come unless I did, so I was asking for his benefit as well as mine.

"Yes. Please. Lloyd," he ground out in time with my thrusts. "You trip. All my. Sensors. Oh, yes. Please."

I thrust up harder into him, reaching deeper, chasing my orgasm, and he cried out. His cock hard in my hand, and

I slid my fist over the head, twisting and pumping, while I was buried to the hilt inside him.

"Oh, Shaun," I gasped. "I'm gonna come."

The surge of pleasure reached its peak and broke, sending wave after wave of orgasm hurtling through me, and his cock began to pulse in my hand. I came so hard, with such force, I almost screamed. It took me a moment to realise Shaun was groaning through his own release.

I let go of his cock and rolled on top of him, still buried deep. I never wanted to leave. I never wanted to stop. I kissed the back of his neck, his shoulder, his nape, behind his ear.

"Are you okay?" I asked.

"I have well surpassed okay."

I smiled and kissed his neck, rocking my hips slowly. I slid in and out, my spent cock still full and keen to go again. It was never-ending with him; the pleasure, the want, the need.

"I could come again," I whispered, kissing down his shoulder. "I've never known such pleasure, Shaun. Only with you."

He spread his legs wide and raised his arse a little. "I do not want you to ever stop."

He didn't just have desires. He loved it. He wanted it. Just as much as me.

I lightly scraped my teeth along his skin and thrust in, long and slow. He moaned that sound that did things to my insides. I was crazy for the noises he made, for the moans and groans, the murmurs, and the way he whispered my name.

I pressed my weight onto his back and kissed the back of his neck. I slid my hands along his and he quickly threaded our fingers, and I made love to him.

"I love being inside you," I whispered. "I love how you feel. I love having you in my bed. I love waking up next to you, I love coming home to you."

He stretched, lifting his arse, giving me more of himself. "Oh, Lloyd," he said, and it sounded like a prayer.

When I came inside him this time, it was slow and deep, but just as powerful. Like something between us heightened, solidified. Became better.

I collapsed on top of him, utterly drained, yet still on a high. I slid out of him and he quickly turned, caging me in his arms and holding me so tight. He put his hand to my cheek, and brought our lips together, kissing me so deeply my eyes rolled back into my head.

Oh boy.

Then he was gone, and when I opened my eyes, he was standing at the side of the bed in all his naked glory. "You have work today. I will run you a shower," he said.

"Or I could just look at you naked all day."

He grinned. "Tempting. Though you should not be late."

I sighed. "What time is it?"

"Six forty-eight," he replied without even thinking. Who knew built-in clocks were so useful. "Are you still tired?"

I rolled over onto my back and stretched. "No. Just a little spent. I'm not complaining though. I could wake up to that every day."

He smiled smugly. "As could I."

Then I remembered that he needed to shower. I'd come in him twice. "Shall I join you in the shower?" I asked. "Or will we shower separately?"

Shaun raised one eyebrow at me. "Rhetorical questions.

A question asked in order to create a dramatic effect or to make a point rather than to get an answer."

I snorted out a laugh. "Point taken." And I followed him into the bathroom.

———————

EVERY DAY that week was the same. I'd go to work, come home to long hugs and tender kisses. We'd talk until dinner time, then I'd grade some papers with his help and input on some matters, and we'd go to bed and make love.

By late Friday night, after a particularly vigorous round of doggy-style sex, then clean-up sex in the shower, we collapsed back on the bed. Shaun was tracing soft patterns on my back, and I began to fall asleep. "What are you mapping out on my back?" I mumbled, not even opening my eyes.

"Nothing," he replied gently, then kissed my temple. Then he did something that sealed the fate of my heart. If it wasn't his before, it certainly was now. He quoted *Moby Dick.*

"'It is not down in any map; true places never are'."

CHAPTER NINE

WE SPENT the weekend doing exactly what normal boyfriends did; reading, cuddling, making out, talking, and laughing. We even went for a walk down to the river while the sun was out. We didn't encounter any other A-Class androids, and either the humans didn't notice us or care, because we were blessedly left to ourselves.

After a few well-spent hours in the bedroom, Shaun was having a shower when the phone rang. True to his word, Myles phoned again on Sunday evening. Caller ID showed SATinc's number and I considered not answering, but with a heavy sigh, I said, "Answer Call."

"Good evening, Mr Salter. Myles Dewegger, SATinc," he began. "How was your second week with your A-Class?"

It grated on me that he didn't use his name. "Very good," I said, aiming for cheerful.

"You were concerned about the instruction manual update," he trailed off.

"Oh yes, that's all sorted, thank you."

There was a brief pause. "Do you... have any concerns or questions?"

"No." I frowned. "I'm very happy."

There was another pause, almost like he wanted to ask or say something but didn't know how to. So I prompted him, "Is there anything else I can help you with?"

"No, no. But if you do have any concerns…"

Why would he keep asking that? Did they know something? Did they somehow know Shaun was different? My eyes shot to the home hub. The source of internet, a wireless tether to SATinc.

"Mr Salter?"

I startled at his voice. "Oh. Yes, thank you, Myles. If I do have any concerns, believe me, I'll be in touch."

"May I ask where your unit is right now?"

Now it was me who paused. "He's having a shower. He needed… cleaning." I cringed, hating that I needed to admit that. There was, after all, only one reason Shaun needed to clean himself. "Why?"

"Oh, no reason. It just sounds very quiet."

"I like silence," I replied. "If you've read my psych report, you'd know that." I didn't care for his tone or what he was implying. "If we're done…"

He went back to using his professional tone. "Yes, of course, Mr Salter. Have a good evening."

The call clicked off just as Shaun walked out. He was freshly showered, his hair brushed neatly, dressed in his pyjamas, looking all domestic and handsome. But there was a cautious look in his eyes, and I knew he must have heard me on the phone. "Everything okay?"

I gave a smile and patted the couch next to me. "Yes. That was just Myles from SATinc, doing his follow-up calls."

Shaun sat down, his back straight. "Did he say anything about me?"

"He wanted to know if I had any concerns," I explained. Shaun turned his head to look at me. "Do you?"

"Actually I do have one concern," I said with a smile. "How am I supposed to go to work this week when all I want to do is stay home with you?"

Shaun visibly relaxed when he realised I was joking. He smiled, and I lay down against him, settling back on his chest, and together we finished reading *Moby Dick*. Then he stroked my hair and we talked about Ishmael and Ahab, and Shaun told me his interpretation of the religious symbolism. This went beyond android behaviour. Far, far beyond it. He wasn't reading some footnotes from an internet essay. He was telling me how it made him feel, how he saw existential religious correlations, and how interpretation is subjective to one's spiritual beliefs.

Did I have any concerns regarding my A-Class unit?

God yes, I did. But not the concerns Myles might assume. Oh, no. My concerns weren't that Shaun's behaviour might be outside his parameters. My concern was what they'd do if they found out.

I stared at the home hub.

Were they listening? Were they watching? Did they have direct access to his CPU?

"Lloyd?" Shaun whispered. "You are distracted. Is anything the matter?"

"No, nothing." I stood up and held out my hand. "I'm tired. Let's go to bed."

I stared at the home hub as I walked past it, and although it was completely futile, I closed my bedroom door behind us. When we were in bed, instead of falling asleep in his arms, I pulled him into mine. He laid his head on my chest and I found his weight soothing. I stroked his hair, as I knew he liked. I relished the silence, the no loud breathing, the no snoring, his warmth, his clean smell. I stared at the ceiling and wondered how on earth I'd ever lived without him before I knew him—and if it ever came down to it, how on earth I'd live without him now—until I fell asleep.

WHEN I SAT in my usual seat at lunch, I waited for Jae to join me. He was a few minutes late, which was nothing new. He did have to walk further from the IT department than I did, but I smiled when he walked in.

He was wearing his usual all-brown attire, carrying a mandarin, he had soup and a rye bread roll. Predictable, predictable, predictable. It was comforting.

He sat down and arranged his tray neatly, then looked up at me and smiled. "How was your weekend?"

"Good. And yours?"

"Yes, the DCC was on all weekend."

"The DCC?"

He looked at me like I was daft. "Digital Chess Championships."

"Oh right."

"Live coverage feeds from all around the world. It was awesome."

I wasn't entirely sure watching computers versus each other playing chess would be riveting. "Sounds it."

He smiled, knowing I thought it was anything but that, and he silently finished his lunch. I watched him as he ate, my finished lunch wrapping neatly folded on my tray. "Jae, may I ask you a question?"

His eyes widened a fraction behind his thick-rimmed glasses. "Sure."

"It's about the home hub unit," I started, not even sure

what I was trying to ask. "Information can stream in, yes. But can information be taken?"

He tilted his head. "You mean uploaded? With or without your permission?"

I glanced quickly around us to make sure no one was paying any attention to us. "Without."

He stared at me for a long, uncomfortable moment. "Home hubs are a unidirectional network, also referred to as a unidirectional security gateway. They're a network device allowing data to travel only in one direction, guaranteeing information security. They're government approved," he said slowly. Then he sat back in his seat and whispered, his lips barely moving, as if he wasn't speaking at all. "Do you think the government is watching?"

"Not the government."

"But someone."

I nodded. "I have... concerns."

He swallowed visibly and looked at someone as they walked to empty their rubbish into the bin. No one could hear us, but his unease worried me. "The unidirectional network is monitored. They might claim it's not, but it has to be."

"Who's they?"

He looked at me like I wasn't following. "The government."

"Why did you say it has to be?"

"Our entire lives are digital. Everything. Since the Russians first shot satellites into space a hundred years ago, there's been a war for information. It's one thing to have satellite imagery of our enemies' military bases, but of our allies too. But guess what happens when every government knows civilian information?" He leaned forward and whispered, "They own us. Financial information, health records, GPS locations in your watch, your phone."

Okay, wow. He was a conspiracy theorist. And I thought I knew him...

He just kept going. "And if that's not bad enough, everything in our homes is connected to and run by the home hub. Did you think the government putting an information gateway in every house in the country was for our benefit?" He shook his head. "So it's one thing that they know you transfer some money, or where you buy all your porn online, what kind of coffee you drink, or that you're getting treatment for an STI. But it also means you can't watch television, search anything on the internet, boil your kettle, or leave your apartment without them knowing."

I let out a low breath. I wasn't prepared for his anti-government or Big Brother tirade but it did work in my favour. "Is there any way to turn off certain appliances? Not turn the appliance off, but turn off their connectivity and keep the appliance on?"

He blinked, clearly surprised by my question. "I don't... that depends. Like your TV? Or your internet browser?" he asked. "If you want to search something online, do it from here. But be aware, nothing illegal. There'll be someone busting down your door before you've logged off."

"It's not my TV or the internet," I admitted, but that wasn't a bad idea. I could do information searches from a library access point. As long as I kept it general... unless SATinc somehow had eyes on my internet activity at work too... I cleared my throat. "What if it was an android?"

He stared, unblinking. His nostrils flared. "What kind of android?"

I considered telling him but stopped myself. "Any.

They're designed to send information back to the AMA if mistreated, right?"

"Yes," he replied cautiously.

"So, can the AMA access information at will?"

Jae studied me for a moment. "Lloyd, has something bad happened to one of your androids? Because that's a federal offence."

"No," I answered quickly. "But what about a manufacturing company? They can download automatic updates to keep their androids abreast of say, traffic law updates, yes?"

He nodded. "Yes."

"Can they upload information from the android? Like, if they wanted to double-check what CPU they were running on?"

Jae stared and blinked, and I knew I'd asked a question that was too specific. He answered quietly. "They'd need internet connectivity, and they say it's a unidirectional network, but I have no doubts it's possible. They watch everything."

I looked around the lunch room to find it almost empty. I asked my next question, looking at the door instead of him. "And if I wanted to disconnect my android from my Wi-Fi?"

"Depending on what kind of android it is; they all have different parameters for how long they could be without internet. But it would eventually shut down, and the AMA would be notified."

I sighed. "That's what I thought."

"I'm going to ignore the specificity and sensitive nature of your questions, Lloyd, and ask if everything's okay? Are you in trouble?" Well, weren't they loaded questions—and ones I apparently didn't have to answer. "I guess you wouldn't have asked otherwise." He leaned in again and whispered, "Don't do anything stupid. They're always watching."

I wasn't sold into his conspiracy theories about the digital war on cybernetics or whatever he thought the government was doing, but there was a truth to his madness. They were watching. Maybe not the government per se, but I was beginning to think SATinc was. They had an vested interest, didn't they? Something about the questions Myles asked, the way he asked them, the way he paused, made me uneasy.

I didn't even trust them to search for information myself. But there was no reason Jae couldn't, was there?

"Can I ask you to search something for me? You have your ear to the ground on these things, right?"

He smiled like I'd just validated his entire existence in his personal war against the digital Goliath. I took it as a yes.

"Can you find out what companies like SATinc have access to? Once an android is registered to a home hub, what can they access?"

His eyes went wide, his mouth fell open. "SATinc?"

I nodded, giving myself away completely. There was no point in hiding it now.

"Holy shit."

"I'd rather no one know," I added. "But—"

"But they're a very big fish in a very small pond."

"I know."

"And you don't trust them."

I shook my head. "No. I don't."

His eyes narrowed. "Leave it with me. I know certain people, certain underground people..."

Oh boy. Was he talking... "Darknet?"

He nodded quickly. "I'll see what I can find out. Might take me a few days."

"That's fine. Thank you."

He left like I'd given him a secret operative mission, and I felt better for having asked. I got through my afternoon classes and couldn't wait to get home. Shaun greeted me with a tight hug, as though he didn't want to let go of me as much I didn't want to let go of him. He rubbed my back, ran his hands over my arse, and gently massaged the knots out of my shoulders. I melted against him, and my God, he felt so damn good. Eventually he pulled back and kissed me softly. "How was your day?"

"Okay," I answered. "How was yours?"

"Quite good," he said, pulling my hand and leading me to the sofa where we sat down. "I cleaned again and ordered your food, and I watched this." He faced the holographic TV screen. "It is most interesting."

I stared at what was on the screen. *Oh boy.* "Home and Away?" I asked, disbelievingly.

"Yes. It is very exciting."

Exciting? Oh boy, indeed.

Home and Away was a drama show that had graced Australian television for eighty years. It was... not exciting. It was woeful. Every possible conceivable plot point had been acted out a thousand times and several characters had died and miraculously reappeared, usually without their memory. It was predictable television trash that was somehow still on TV.

"I was scrolling through channels," Shaun said, "and saw there were androids acting."

Oh, of course. "Yes. It's a scripted show to depict real life."

"This android in particular is named Alf. He has a very unusual vernacular."

I smiled. "Is that right?"

"Yes," Shaun answered seriously. Then he pointed to the screen, where a blonde woman was frozen mid-pause. "And that is Sharon. She is human. Her best friend and her ex-husband have been having a secret sexual relationship. Alf has befriended the ex-husband and knows about the affair. Sharon wants Alf to disclose information, but Alf cannot cause harm or lie to humans. He does not want to hurt his friend, yet he has to answer Sharon honestly. It is quite the conundrum."

I fought a smile. "Yes, I can see how it might be."

"Is something funny?"

"No," I lied. "You're just being completely adorable."

"Adorable. Inspiring great affection or delight."

I leaned in and kissed him. "Yes. There are a lot of movies with androids and plenty of TV shows. We can make a list if you want. It never occurred to me that you'd like to identify with characters on TV."

"Social representation of all groups is important."

"Yes, it really is. We can watch one later if you like." I took his hand. "Did you want to go for a walk? You've been cooped up in here all day."

He was quiet for a few seconds, like he was thinking of his answer. "Yes. I think I would like to take a walk."

I put my coat back on and Shaun slipped into his and we walked down toward the river. It was getting dark, though the sky was cloudless, the night cold and clear. Passers-by mostly kept their heads down and collars up, minding their own business. But Shaun looked around bright-eyed and curious, like always, keen to take everything in and learn. He held his hand out, wanting me to hold it, and I happily threaded our fingers.

While we were out in the open, I took the opportunity to speak freely. If SATinc could hear directly by somehow relaying his recurrent networks and audial feeds, I had no idea, but I hated the idea of keeping things from him.

"I spoke to Jae today. He's a friend at work who specialises in IT. He's very attuned to all things internet related. He has friends who are able to find out information no one else can obtain. I asked him to find out what he can on SATinc."

Shaun paused. "Why? If you want to know something, I can access any information online."

"This information won't be readily available on the internet. It's on what's called the darknet."

He paused for a second. "Darknet. Any overlay network that can be accessed only with specific software, configurations, or authorisation, often using non-standard communications protocols."

"Yes. Secret stuff. Yes, like if SATinc is capable of accessing your processing unit and taking data without your consent."

Shaun nodded. "And you trust your friend Jae?"

"I do. He has some weird theories about how much the government oversees, so he knows about secrecy. He said it might take a few days."

"What do we do in the meantime?"

"We carry on like there's nothing wrong. We act like they'd expect us to act."

Shaun gave me his crooked smile. "Would they expect us to go home and for you to see just how many of my internal sensors you can activate at once?"

I barked out a laugh. "I think that might be expected, yes."

He turned back for home. "Then I would hate to disappoint them."

I DIDN'T SEE Jae the next day, though I did look for him. Someone said they'd seen him earlier but there was some software issue in the science department that took priority. I was a little disappointed, but I trusted that if Jae had any information to give me, he'd find me.

When I got home, I was greeted with my usual, and very welcome, long hug from Shaun. He met me just inside the door and slid his arms around me and buried his face in my neck. "I missed you today," he murmured. Then he pulled back and kissed me. "Did you speak to Jae?"

I put my finger to my lips and shook my head, then nodded toward the home hub. "No, he was busy."

Shaun blinked and his brow furrowed. He walked to the table, picked up a notepad and pen, then sat on the sofa. "I have cleaned today," he said, his voice a little stilted, robotic. "And I enjoyed more *Home and Away*. Poor Alf is in quite the predicament and Sharon is being rather unpleasant..." He continued to tell me about the episodes of the silly show he enjoyed while he wrote on a notepad.

I sat beside him and he handed it to me.

Is his absence something that should concern us?

My gaze shot to his. "I'm sure Alf will find a way out of it. He can't lie or hide the truth, so I'm sure in the end, it will all work out," I said as I wrote my reply. *No. There was a tech emergency. All is well.*

"I'm sure you are correct," he said, answering both conversations. "Are you hungry? I can get your dinner."

I leaned in and kissed him. "Dinner sounds great."

I took the notepad and followed him into the kitchen. The fact he'd used initiative and creativity to even think to use a silent, analogue way to communicate was incredibly clever. And well and truly outside of android parameters. And did he use a contraction just now?

"I think I feel like vegetables tonight," I said while I wrote on the notepad. *Clever use of pen and paper.*

He took the vegetable dinner from the fridge, grinned at me, and kissed me with smiling lips. He placed the meal in the oven and quickly wrote on the paper. *Thank you.* Then writing messages became our thing. During dinner, afterwards, watching TV. He seemed to find it exciting and amusing. *Now we've finished* Moby Dick, *would you like to select a new novel for us to read?*

Oh. I totally wasn't expecting that. *Would you like to choose?*

Shaun could write so much faster than me. His hand flew over the page so fast. *I think I would like to reread* Moby Dick.

I also wasn't expecting that.

Then he added, *Though you have read it many times and may not wish to read it again so soon.*

I took the notepad, and he waited patiently for me to write. *I'll happily reread if you want to. I love it.*

He took the notepad and pen and hesitated. He put the nib to the page several times and obviously thought about what he wanted to write. *Why do you love it?*

I took the pen. *It's a literary masterpiece.*

His brow creased and he wrote quickly. *Love indicates emotional attachment, therefore it makes you feel.*

Yes. Reading elicits many emotions. I get great enjoyment out of it.

He took the notepad back and held the pen poised, and he seemed to think for a long moment, then put his pen down and slowly put the notepad on the coffee table.

"Shaun?"

He looked at me and sat back, his hands fisted on his thighs. For the first time in a long time, he looked... like an android.

"What's wrong?"

He glanced at the home hub and shook his head. I picked up the notepad and pen and handed it back to him.

He stared at me for a long, long moment, then wrote three words that changed everything.

What is love?

CHAPTER TEN

GOD, how did it come to this? I wasn't expecting this. Not ever again. It was one thing to know I was in love. I'd admitted that to myself already, but to admit it to Shaun... to an android? An android who was never supposed to be anything more than company. Someone for me to talk to, to save me from being alone.

To save me.

This wasn't a conversation to be scrawled on paper. I looked at the home hub. "Playlist Classical." Mozart began to play. "Volume Up."

I took Shaun's hand and went into our room, closing the door behind us. I had no idea if playing music would have any effect if SATinc could listen. For all I knew, they could hear me through Shaun. And if that was the case, then it was hopeless because this had to be said.

"Love is..."

He spoke when my voice trailed away. "I understand there can be a variety of related but distinct meanings in different contexts. I understand the Greek history from eros and agape. I know that sciences like psychology, anthropol-

ogy, neuroscience, and biology have added to the understanding of the concept of love. I can read any definition in
any language, Lloyd. I can quote poetry and science, but I
cannot quantify the... there is an emotional equation that I
cannot determine an answer to."

Oh boy.

I sat on my bed and waited for him to sit next to me,
then looked into his eyes. "Shaun, love isn't logical. There's
no formula."

He frowned slowly. "I am conflicted."

Oh hell. He was confused, trying to solve the complexi-
ties of human emotion like a mathematical equation.
"Shaun, did something happen? To make you feel
this way?"

"On *Home and Away*, Sharon told Ridge she loved him.
He did not return it and she became unreasonable."

Oh. God. Of course it was from that stupid TV show. It
couldn't have been for me... he's an android. Disappoint-
ment and shame snuffed out any hope, and my heart felt
like concrete.

Shaun's eyebrows furrowed. "And you speak of books
and of literature in general with such fondness. And tonight
you tell me you love it."

I nodded, not sure I trusted myself to speak.

"I have tried to understand what love could mean," he
whispered. "A-Class androids are fitted with synthetic
chemical reactions to replicate oxytocin and vasopressin."
Then he spoke like he was quoting some research paper.
"Released during sex and heightened by skin-to-skin
contact, oxytocin deepens feelings of attachment and makes
couples feel closer to one another after sexual relations.
Oxytocin provokes feelings of contentment, calmness, and
security, which are often associated with mate bonding.

Vasopressin has been linked to behaviour that produces long-term, monogamous relationships. In addition to the positive feelings romance brings, love also deactivates the neural pathway responsible for negative emotions, such as fear and social judgement. These positive and negative feelings involve two neurological pathways. The one linked with positive emotions connects the prefrontal cortex to—"

I put my hand up to stop him. "Shaun. I know this. What are you trying to say?"

"That I am unsure of my A-Class stature. You have expressed concerns that I may be over and above what they reasoned an A-Class is capable of, and I agree. In my ability to adapt or read social cues, but also in my ability to feel. I can quote medical or scientific findings on emotional responses, but I know what they are because I feel them."

Oh boy. My heart rate took off, something he clearly didn't miss.

"What makes you react in such a way?" he asked. "Does your pulse quicken from fear? Or is it excitement? Because I am uncertain of many things at this time. I am trying to understand…"

I took his face in my hands and kissed him. When I pulled back, I put my forehead to his. "Shaun, I feel many things right now too. Uncertainty of our future, fear of what that might mean. But there's also excitement and joy, happiness."

He tilted his head slightly. "I don't follow."

"You wanted to know what love is, well, it's all of those things. It's everything you said about chemical reactions and it's an entire vortex of other emotions. Shaun, I don't know what the A-Class—if that's even what you are—is capable of or what they were aiming for by developing an android so advanced, but I know this: I love you. I'm in love with you,

Shaun. Android or not, A-Class or not. It doesn't matter to me." I kissed him softly. "I love *you*."

My God, it felt so good to say it. To tell him. I understood in that very moment it didn't matter if he could never say it back, or if the only love he understood was a synthetic, programmed version of the real thing. Love was a gift to give and should be given without expecting anything in return.

He stared at me, blinked, and then a slow smile spread across his face. "You do?"

I nodded. "Yes."

"Because this conflicted neural network issue I appear to be experiencing becomes more apparent when I think about you." He took my hand. "My synapses seem to fire more quickly, and my internal temperature rises point zero-eight degrees when I recall the way you laugh or when you touch me. I experience elevated synthetic dopamine and oxytocin levels, only I cannot determine if it is synthetic or real, because it feels very real."

"Shaun, what are you saying?"

"I am acutely aware of my existentialism. I know why I am here. I know I am not human and I know the differences between us are more than simply physical. But Lloyd, I feel these things. Synthetic or not, I feel them. And if love is everything you say it is, that it is not logical or even reasonable, then I can only conclude that what I feel for you, when I think of you, when I am with you, is love."

I blinked. *He loved me. He loves me.* I'd hoped... I'd longed... but I never dreamed it was possible. Tears welled in my eyes and I barked out a breath.

"Why do you react in such a way?" Shaun asked. He looked to the floor, a frown etched on his face. "Does this not make you happy? I was not prepared for unrequited—"

I lifted his chin and kissed him. Then I climbed over

and straddled him, kissing him deeply and wrapping my arms around him. He responded and laid down on the bed, but he was hesitant and eventually held me back so my face was an inch from his.

"Lloyd."

I brushed his hair off his forehead and stared into his blue, blue eyes. "I love you, Shaun. What you feel is not unrequited. I wasn't laughing or mocking you. My reaction was relief. A lifetime of relief."

"A lifetime?"

"I've always been alone. No one's ever understood me, not like you. I have... quirks that some find difficult to put up with."

"You don't like hearing people eat or breathe. Or noise. Or mess."

Again, with a contraction. I nodded. "Yes."

He studied my eyes and the corner of his lips curled into a smile. "Then lucky you have me."

I laughed. "I really am."

His smile faded into something serious and he traced his thumb across my cheek. "What I feel is still conflicting, I cannot lie."

"In a good way?"

"I believe so, yes."

I pecked his lips with mine. "Love is confusing."

"And exhilarating. And overwhelming. And..."

"And?"

"And I have an unexplainable desire to be naked with you. More than I've experienced previously."

I chuckled and kissed him slowly. "Is that so?"

"I want to feel your skin on mine. I want your chest pressed against mine; I want to bury my face in your neck and feel your arms around me. I want to touch you and have you hold me. Not for sexual release—well, not only for sex—but to satisfy a different need. A need that has been building since I met you. This need I've deduced may in fact be love. I need to express with my body. I cannot explain that."

"Do you want to express it with your body right now?"

He nodded. "Very much."

So he did, and it was utterly glorious. It was slow and tender, fraught with passion so raw, so intense it took my breath away. And when he'd impaled himself on me and I brought us both to climax, he came like never before.

His cock pulsed like it always did, but his reaction was new. He arched his back, his whole body went rigid, and he let out a silent scream. Then he held me so damn tight, wrapped around me like a glove, and nuzzled into me until I fell asleep. I dreamed of birds flying free and cute kittens playing, the sound of Shaun's laughter as Mozart chimed in the background. I dreamed of a future, of love, and being at sea with *Moby Dick* and even through the wildest storm, Ishmael kept me safe.

I woke up anchored to Shaun. He was lying with his head on my chest, my arm around his shoulder.

"Good morning," he said gently. "I was going to wake you for work, but I would much rather you stay in bed with me."

I smiled and stroked his hair, how I knew he liked it. "What time is it?"

"Nine minutes past seven."

I stretched out and slid my arm back around him for a quick cuddle before I had to get up. "I wish I could stay here with you," I murmured.

"Yes, who decided that humans needed to work? I would like to write them a strongly worded letter."

I chuckled and kissed the top of his head. "Shower with me."

He looked up at me, grinning. "If I have to." He commando rolled off the bed and had the water running before I could sit up.

I TRIED to contain my edginess when I saw Jae walk into the lunchroom. He had his usual soup and mandarin on a tray and slid into the seat across from me. "I wondered if you'd be in today," I said, folding and ironing flat my lunch wrapper with my fingers.

He took a spoonful of soup. "Yeah, sorry. Got caught up yesterday with line issues in the science department."

"Get everything sorted out?"

He nodded. "About that thing you asked me to look into." Another spoonful of soup. My guess was he was going for pretence in case someone was watching. *God, when did I get so paranoid?* "I have some friends in Singapore and Taiwan who know people who work for the sister company."

I knew who he meant. ATAinc, or Android Technology Asia, was a sister division of SATinc. "And?"

"They said the company protocols are global, so there's reason to believe if it happens there, it can happen here."

"What happens?"

"I asked what kind of access they have when an android is registered through the home hub." He ate more of his soup. "Anyway, after they stopped laughing, they said complete."

"Complete access?"

Jae nodded again and finished his soup while I got my head around what that meant.

"Can they upload diagnostics on things such as CPUs and battery health? That kind of thing?" I asked.

"Probably. They can upload all health stats and diagnostics and see how it's running. Whether that gives mainframe data or just running capabilities... well, before today, I wouldn't believe they could know that without actually accessing the android, physically. But now I'm not sure." Then he waved his hand dismissively. "But I'm not talking about the android, Lloyd. I mean complete access to you. They can now see your grocery order, what movies you watch, when you use your key card to leave your apartment."

I didn't give a damn what they could see about me. I needed to know what they could see about Shaun.

"They're not supposed to," he went on to say. "By law, I mean. They *are* supposed to run on a unidirectional network, secure from hackers and all that bullshit. But if they wanted to spy? Hell yes, they could."

"Would they? Do you think they'd risk it?"

He shrugged. "Depends on what's at stake? And for a little guy like you? I'd be thinking no."

"Little guy?"

He snorted. "Compared to the military or the Australian Defence Force, yeah."

"What do you mean?"

"Well, they have androids in the military, right?"

"Yes. And police force."

"Right. So they send in androids to foreign countries, into foreign armies. I mean, they make these androids for other countries, right?"

"Military grade, yes."

"Well, imagine if they used multidirectional networks?" He leaned in and whispered, "Imagine if they could upload data on what the android sees, hears. They'd have implanted spies in every country..." He shook his head and let out a slow breath. "This is huge, Lloyd. This is bigger than I ever thought about."

Oh boy.

Then his eyes narrowed at me. "Just what kind of android do you have?"

So here it was. I could lie or deflect or tell him not to worry about it, but he was helping me and surely I owed him the truth. "An A-Class. Android, not gynoid."

I just outed myself.

His eyes widened, followed by his smile. "Wow."

I cleared my throat. "Yes, wow."

"I've read reviews. All five-star, I might add." Then he stopped, his smirk disappeared, and he sat up straight. "Wait. You think they're spying on you through your android?"

Clearly the fact I liked men and not women didn't even rate as interesting, much less the fact I was technosexual. "I'm not sure. They've asked some rather peculiar follow-up questions that raised a little red flag for me."

"What kind of questions?"

"Repeating questions like they're trying to catch me out. They ask me if I'm happy with my purchase and if I believe everything is running okay, any unusual behaviour."

Jae tilted his head. "That is peculiar." Then he pointed his finger at me. "You know, I read something online about the A-Class the other week. Something to do with a frame-work and an error code. I didn't read the article because it wasn't of interest to me then. I'll see if I can find it for you. Maybe they're trying to ask without admitting there was an error somewhere. Like maybe the framework error makes an android speak random Spanish or something."

I was all for honesty to a point, but there was no way I was telling that Shaun was performing far beyond his android capabilities. "Hmm, maybe. Hopefully that's all it is."

"I can ask around, see if there's any more to it," he added.

"What do you suggest I do about my home hub?"

"Leave it be for now. If they can't reach you or communicate with your android, it'll only raise suspicions."

"True."

He checked his watch. "Shoot. I gotta go."

"Yes, I should too."

"I'll be in touch," he said, hurrying out the door.

WHEN I GOT HOME, Shaun stood up from the sofa and crossed the room in long strides to collect me in a crushing hug. "Hey," I said in greeting. But he didn't let me go. He nuzzled my neck and held me tighter. "Everything okay?"

He shook his head. "No."

I pulled back so I could see his face. "Shaun, what is it?"

He frowned, and sadness coloured his eyes. "I discovered the movie channels today," he whispered. "The android selection, as you suggested."

I thought it might be good for him to see characters he could identify with. I almost smiled at his reaction. "And? Did you not enjoy it?"

His lip trembled. "No."

Oh my God. I took his face in my hands. "Jesus, Shaun, what happened? Why are you upset?"

"The movie was called *Frailty*, in the drama section. I should have realised." His frown deepened. "The human was a lady called June. And she acquired an android for uses around the home, like that of a husband: heavy lifting and climbing ladders. His name was Harold and they became best friends."

"Okay," I hedged.

"As the years went on, Harold saw June through many aspects of her life and they loved each other very much. Through illness and social discrimination because people didn't understand how they could be in love. But they never faltered. They stayed together through it all. She became elderly, Lloyd. She grew old, and he did not. He never changed, he never aged." His chin quivered. "And June passed away, leaving Harold all alone."

Oh boy.

He had just realised that he's, in fact, immortal, and I'm not. I would age, I would have illnesses, and I would eventually leave him forever.

Still, with my hands to his face, I pulled him in for a kiss, then slid my arms around him. I rubbed his back, his hair, his nape, I swayed us a little, and I held him even tighter. What could I possibly say? He'd just recognised love and death in the space of twenty-four hours. What could I possibly say that would fix that? There was nothing. He would have to live without me at some point.

"I do not want to lose you," he mumbled into my shirt collar.

"I know you don't."

"I won't." He shook his head. "Lloyd, I cannot."

I pulled back and kissed him softly. "I am human," I whispered. "I won't be here forever."

"I know." He frowned again, but the sadness in his eyes

was now replaced with determination. "And when that moment comes, I will deactivate."

Now it was me who tilted my head. "You'll what?"

"I have a self-deactivation sequence. I will enable that and deactivate."

I blinked. "Isn't that permanent?"

"Yes. Much like your death will be."

He was going to kill himself? "Shaun, no," I whispered, shaking my head. "You can't."

"Why not?"

"Because... because you can live forever. What if you find someone else to live with?"

He looked horrified. No, not horrified. He looked offended. "I would never. Not as I have with you. Do not ask that of me. I might not have the intricacies and subtleties of a human heart, Lloyd. But what I feel is real to me."

I took a hold of his face again, a little harder this time. "That's not what I meant. I wasn't discrediting what you feel or your ability to love. I would never. I love you, Shaun. And I love that you love me. It's the best thing to ever happen to me. *You* are the best thing to ever happen to me." I kissed him soundly. "I just meant that, one day, many years after, you may learn to love again. With someone new."

He shook his head. "No. I'm not a character from *Moby Dick*, Lloyd. I would not be as Ishmael was. I wouldn't survive it, while all I lived for disappears under the surface."

"Oh, Shaun." I kissed him again and rested my forehead on his and we both took a long moment to absorb everything. Eventually, I said, "If it's your decision, then I'll respect it."

"Thank you."

After a long time, I took his hand and led him to the

kitchen. I didn't want to eat or drink, I just wanted to lean against something while I held him for hours. I never wanted to let him go. So we stood there in each other's arms and held one another.

He never asked if I'd spoken to Jae or if I knew any more on what SATinc might be privy to, and I certainly didn't bring it up.

Instead, I told him I loved him and held him tighter.

———

JAE WAS CALLED out again for the day, which was often the case. Though he left a note at the admin desk for me. "Waiting on more information," the B-Class gynoid said pleasantly.

"Was there any other information?" I asked her.

"No. Message complete. Have a nice day."

I thanked her and went on my way. Jae was waiting on more information. More information on what exactly, was anyone's guess.

I was halfway through my last class of the day when my phone buzzed in my pocket. And then it buzzed again. The entire class went quiet, and when the students realised it was my phone, there were a few sniggers and I told them to shush. I pulled out my phone, seeing a missed call and a message from the last person I ever expected to call me at work. It was Shaun. He was to only ever call in an emergency. *Damnit, why did I have it switched to silent?*

"Play Message."

Shaun's voice came through the phone. "Lloyd. Something's wrong. Please come home."

I felt the blood drain from my face and looked up at the class. None of them were laughing now. "Class dismissed."

I grabbed my bag and ran for my car. I didn't wait for my driver to ask me for my destination. "Home. And please hurry. It's an emergency."

He looked at me with his never-changing expression, his always pleasant smile. "Shall I notify the police, ambulance, or fire station?"

"None. Just drive. Please."

CHAPTER ELEVEN

I RACED FROM THE CAR, took the too-slow lift to my floor, and ran to my apartment. I had no clue what to expect. I had no clue what was wrong. I shoved the door open, almost dropped my messenger bag, and found Shaun pacing.

He looked a mess. Well, not his usual pristine self. His hair was shaggy, like he'd run his hand through it a hundred times, his shirt was half-unbuttoned, half-untucked. His belt was on the sofa... was his fly undone?

"Shaun, what's wrong?"

He stopped pacing, looked at me, and went back to pacing.

It was then I noticed the television. Oh dear Lord, he'd found the eight hundred channels. More specifically, he'd found the 870s, which was gay pornography dedicated for technosexuals. It was android sex: humans with androids, androids with androids... I should know. I'd watched a lot of it.

Shaun was still pacing. "Lloyd. Lloyd."

I rushed over to him and put my hands on his arms to get him to at least stop moving. "Shaun, what's wrong?"

"Propagation function error. Too much input. Input overload."

I stared at him, then glanced at the TV. Porn was still playing, and a man had his android bent over a bed, taking him from behind. There was groaning and moaning, sex sounds, and grunting. Then I noticed the lube on the dining table, and his fly was undone. "Did you try and..."

"Attempted sensory output failed."

Oh boy. He'd gotten himself into a state because he watched porn. I mean, it was almost comical. Until I realised it wasn't a laughing matter.

Shaun twitched, and his voice was robotic. "Diagnostic check, input data and sensory error code 85100."

Oh my God. He was in serious danger of overloading. "Shaun tell me what to do!"

"Input overload."

"I need your control panel. What does that code mean?" I ran to the cabinet and powered up the control panel. "Search error code 85100."

The screen blinked, then showed me the answer. Input overload error—requires sensory output or power unit down to reset.

I looked up at Shaun. "Do you need to shut down?"

His eyes went wide and he shook his head, like fear struck him at the thought. "Negative. Negative. Input overload."

Now I was on the verge of panicking. He'd once asked me to never shut him down, and I promised I wouldn't. Unless it was for his own safety. But there was no way I was going to reset him. I didn't know what 'restore to factory default settings' meant for him. Would the Shaun I knew and loved be gone forever? "It says you require sensory output. How do I do that?"

He pointed to the television, to the men having sex. "Sensory output required."

Sensory output. He'd told me before about his sensors requiring output signals when he'd joked about needing sex.

"You need sex?"

He palmed his dick. "Input overload."

Oh. My. God.

Of course! He couldn't come unless I did. He'd been watching porn for hours probably, activating his sensory input with no chance of output. He'd tried to masturbate but he couldn't reach orgasm without me.

"You need to come."

He seemed to sigh with relief. "Lloyd. Please. Input data and sensory error code 85100."

"Okay," I said, sliding my face along his jaw. "It's okay. You'll be fine." I pressed myself against him and I could feel his hard-on. Which was new, wasn't it? He was only supposed to be turned on if I was turned on, but he was definitely a lot harder than me. Then he slid his hand between us and palmed my dick. Knowing he needed me, literally needed me, was a heady feeling, and knowing I'd be inside him soon coupled with the pornographic sex sounds in the background, I was getting hard in no time.

But this wasn't just about my need. This time, it was more about his. "The quickest way for sensory output is to activate all your sensors, yes?"

His voice was a pleading whisper. "Confirmed."

I pulled him in for a hard kiss. "Then get on your knees."

He blinked, then knelt in front of me. I took off my jacket and threw it onto the sofa, and when I reached for the lube on the dining table, he pulled at my belt. I looked down and he was looking up at me while he expertly undid my belt and popped my fly. I took my semi-erection out from my briefs and slicked myself with lube, getting myself harder.

I didn't even have to tell him to open his mouth.

He just leaned forward, opened his lips wide with a mix of pleading and desperation in his eyes. "Oh, Shaun." I pressed my cockhead into his mouth and felt the nudge of his throat opening, so I pushed further in, feeling the pop of him taking the head. "Oh, God."

He slid his hands around my thighs and rocked back and forth on me taking me deeper into his throat, his lips closed around me. The suction of the Fleshjack, the ribbing, felt so, so good.

But he'd need more than just this. He needed all his internal sensors activated. I pulled out of his mouth and he looked up at me, confused, scared. I traced my thumb across his bottom lip which slid with lube, like lip gloss. I couldn't resist the urge to bend down and kiss him, plunging my tongue into his mouth. "Now get up and lean over the table."

He shot to his feet, fluid and lightning fast. He undid his pants, and pressing his thighs to the dining table, he leaned across it. I pulled his trousers over his arse cheeks, then his briefs, just down far enough so I could see the small opening of his arse.

He was glorious.

I didn't apply more lube. I didn't wait a second. I just aligned my cock up to his hole and pushed all the way in.

Shaun moaned, long and loud. The men and androids on the television moaned and someone came, their cries of ecstasy a beautiful soundtrack to what we were doing. I leaned over his back, buried inside him to the hilt, and thrust harder, harder, harder. "Is that what you need?"

"Con. Firm. Ed."

I groaned, pushing in as far as I could. His feet lifted off the floor with every thrust; he moaned and gripped the far edge of the table as I took him. He needed to come, and so God help me, I'd make him.

"You want me to come?"

"Conf. Irmed. Lloyd. Please."

I pushed and thrust, chasing my orgasm to the brink of oblivion and Shaun arched his back and groaned, almost a scream, as I came inside him. He jerked and shuddered beneath me and I collapsed on top of him, my face in his shoulder blade, until the room stopped spinning.

He was quiet and still, and the weight of what I'd just done to him settled over me. "Are you okay?"

I was almost afraid to hear his answer.

"System input levels are moderate to high."

I pulled out of him and stood up straight, waiting for him to do the same. His pants were around his thighs, mine were still up over my hips but open to reveal my half-hard, glistening dick.

He... he was still hard.

"Moderate to high? What does that mean?" I asked. He wasn't speaking like a robot anymore, that had to be a good sign. "You're sounding better."

"Diagnostic check confirms levels are no longer catastrophic."

"Catastrophic?"

"Catastrophic, meaning system overload and shutdown is imminent."

I put my hands on his arms, then cupped his face. "We can't ever get to catastrophic again." He glanced at the television, where two androids were now having sex, so I said, "Television Off."

The room went silent.

I looked down between us, at his still hard dick. "You said your input levels were still high. What does that mean?"

"More output is required."

"More sex?"

"I liked your theory to activate all my sensors," he said. Then he gave the smallest smirk. "Perhaps we need to activate all my sensors again?"

I grabbed his face, half-frustrated, half-amused, and kissed him. "You scared the hell out of me."

His smile faded. "I too, was afraid. I was not able to control the situation."

"No more porn. No more watching any of the channels in the 800s. Unless I'm here with you, okay?"

He nodded. "I do apologise. I was unsure if I should call you at work, but I could not control my output senses."

"I'm glad you called me at work. I'd hate to think what would have happened if you'd gone into mandatory shutdown."

He tilted his head. "You were going to power me down?"

"I was worried. I thought it might reset your input and outputs and that would fix you." I swallowed hard. "But you made me promise not to do that."

He frowned again. "I do not want to be shutdown. Being in an unconscious state scares me."

I kissed him, then slid my arms around him just to hold him. His still-hard cock pressed against my hip. "You still need more output," I whispered.

"Yes. Safe levels are low to moderate."

"Then we better go to bed, yes?"

He smiled. "Affirmative."

I squeezed his arse cheek. "I like it when you speak all android."

He chuckled. "Internal sensor activation required. Multiple applications may be necessary." He made a start for the bedroom but stopped, grabbed the lube with a smirk, and went on his way. "Wait times not to be imposed." Then he stopped at the hallway and turned back to face me. "That means don't make me wait, Lloyd."

I snorted out a laugh. "Yeah, I got that. Thanks."

I unbuttoned my shirt as I followed him, toeing out of my shoes at the door. Shaun was now completely naked, standing beside the bed. His cock was still fully hard, his hair in even more disarray than before. He slowly wrapped his hand around his cock and stroked. "How would you like me?"

I stared at his ministrations. "Does that make you feel good?" I asked.

He didn't stop. "Yes. But I am unable to climax without you. I tried today, but it did not work."

"Did you like watching the porn?"

"Yes. It was visually and physically stimulating."

"But it overstimulated you, and your output systems almost overheated."

"Yes." He kept stroking. "I found the channels quite by accident. I did not search for it on purpose. Once I started watching, I was unable to stop. I became stimulated and then I became..."

I stepped in close and slid my hand over his, feeling his cock slide between our fingers. "I was of the impression androids couldn't become aroused on their own."

"That is true. Normal androids cannot."

"But you can."

"I am not a normal android."

"No, you're not," I whispered, then ever so slowly, I went to my knees in front of him. I looked up at him, and opening my mouth, I guided his cockhead onto my tongue.

"Lloyd," he said, his voice strained. "Overstimulation when sensory input is already high is not recommended."

Oh. I licked up the underside of his shaft and under the head before standing up. "Do you need more sensory output first?"

He nodded. "Please."

"Then get on the bed and lie on your stomach, legs spread."

He did as I asked and, laid out like that, all spread and naked, he was so beautiful. He turned his head to watch me finish undressing, so I made a show of adding a little more lube to my cock and giving myself a few strokes. "I'm always hard for you," I murmured.

He pushed his forehead into the mattress and raised his arse a little. "System input levels are moderate to high," he replied. "Delay is not recommended."

I crawled onto the bed and up over his body. I kissed his shoulder and pressed my cock into his arse crack, sliding between his cheeks. "I won't be as rough this time," I whispered into the back of his neck. "But I'll be in just as deep."

He whined, a low guttural sound that mimicked impatience and frustration and possibly system failure if I overstimulated him again. So I readjusted my hips, aligned my cock at his hole, and sank into him.

"Oh God, Shaun." I ran my hands through his hair and thrust into him, long and slow. He lifted his arse even higher, giving me more of him. "Is that deep enough?" I asked, biting back the desire to slam into him.

"Yes," he mumbled. "Affirmative."

I pulled out, almost all the way, then pushed all the way back in. And when I was in to the hilt, I rolled my hips over and over, making him groan. Then I stopped, dead still, just feeling every sensation of being inside him. "I want to stay in you forever. But you need to come again, don't you?"

"Yes, Lloyd. Please." He bucked his hips back and forth, trying to ride my cock. He needed more, he was getting desperate, and that gave me an idea. I pulled out of him, all the way, and knelt back on my haunches. He turned around. "Lloyd, no. Please."

"I want to give you more," I explained. "You have full knowledge of the positions for sex?"

"Yes."

"Then sixty-nine me. I want to activate all your internal sensors at once."

He didn't need telling twice. He quickly slid into position so we were both on our sides, his face at my cock, and mine at his. I had barely got myself comfortable when he slid my cock into his throat.

"Holy shit," I cried, taking a second to acclimatise to the pleasure. Then I took his cock into my mouth, activating his penile sensors. Then I fingered his arse, activating his internal anal sensors. My cock was already working his internal throat sensors. He started to hum and vibrate, and I wondered if it was too much for him, if there was a risk of overstimulating him all at once, if his sensory drives would overload... but then he fondled my balls and traced my perineum and the vibrations running through him reverberated around my cock, and it was all just too much.

His cock pulsed in my mouth just I shot into his throat, and the both of us clung to each other while our orgasms rocketed through us. Pleasure strung from every nerve as I convulsed and writhed, and it took a long while before any semblance of thought returned to my mind. Finally I pulled away. "Are you okay?"

No answer.

"Shaun?"

Nothing.

I sat up and moved to his face. He had a glazed-over, blissful look on his face. "Shaun!" I gently tapped his face, and he began to smile.

"Sensory input is still high," he whispered. "You may need to repeat that process."

I sagged with relief. "Oh my God, you scared me! I thought I broke you!"

He barked out a laugh, then shot up and encased me in his arms before landing back on the bed, his face above mine. The light was back in his eyes, his usual smile in place. "Thank you."

"I take it your input and output levels are back to within the normal range."

"Yes, thank you." He leaned down and kissed me. "Experiencing input overload may almost be worth it if you'd do that to me again."

I laughed. "Oh, I can do that to you again, but no more input overloads, okay?"

He was still smiling beautifully. "Okay." He stared into my eyes. "I love you."

I touched the side of his face. "I love you too."

He leaned into my hand. "I apologise again for calling you at work."

"It's fine." I kissed the tip of his nose. "You sure you feel better now?"

Shaun nodded. "I think I shall only read books. Television only seems to disrupt my neural pathways." Then his brow furrowed. "My brain... my CPU—"

"Your brain."

The corner of his mouth twitched in an almost-smile. "My brain," he said again, "Doesn't appear to be compatible with television."

I ran my nose along his jaw and kissed him there softly. "I don't think it's an incompatibility issue. I think you interpret more than they allowed for with your processor."

He looked at me quizzically. "How so?"

"Whatever makes you different, makes you better than they allowed for." I shrugged. "Maybe a normal android can watch television without concern, but you internalise, interpret and understand as a human would. It's only the complexity of humanity that eludes you."

He closed his eyes and whispered, "I am not human."

"You're better than human." His eyes shot open, and I smiled as I held his face. "Humans—not all humans, but most—stopped caring a long time ago. People became detached. Interacting online became normal because interacting with humans and all the nonsense, effort, and trivial drama that came with it became too difficult. It was easier to speak to our friends online when we wanted, then close down the internet when we needed silence. Androids became commonplace and it was easy; companionship without unnecessary drama."

I sighed loudly and cupped his face. "So you internalise and interpret what you see on television, and where a human would disregard it, you do not. Because you care, because you're a good... person."

"I'm not a person."

"Yes, you are."

"I am an android."

"You are a person to me."

He stared at me for a long while until his small smile turned shy and then became a grin. "Thank you." He kissed me, still smiling. "You must be hungry. Let me fix you dinner."

"Should you shower first?"

He stopped. "Oh, yes," he said, disappointed. "I wish to get you dinner also. You could wait, or you could shower with me?"

I chuckled and kissed his frowning lips. "You go shower. I can get my own dinner. When you're done in the shower, you can join me at the dinner table, okay?"

He was in the shower by the time I'd pulled on pants and a sweater, and no sooner had I set the table and put my meal on the placemat, than he joined me. Wearing neatly pressed pyjama pants and a matching top, his hair wet and neatly brushed. He looked immaculate and beautiful. He sat down next to me and smiled, opening his mouth to say something just as the phone rang.

I glanced at the holographic screen. The caller ID flashed, and I took Shaun's hand. "It's SATinc," I said.

His eyes were wide and he looked a little scared. I squeezed his hand. "Answer Call."

The line clicked and Myles Dewegger's voice was loud and clear. "Mr Salter," he began. "We have had an abnormal reading with your A-Class today."

I stared at Shaun but answered Myles. "Is that so?"

"Yes. High level input error codes.

Jesus. They knew. Of course they did. I had to play this down without giving anything away about Shaun's abilities. "Oh yes, that was my mistake. I do apologise."

"Your mistake?"

"Yes. Are you familiar with edging?"

Silence.

I cringed. "Sexual edging is to bring someone to the brink of... climax." I cleared my throat. "Without permitting release. Many times. It was supposed to be enjoyable. I wasn't aware it would affect him like that."

Shaun raised an eyebrow at me, but I put my finger to my lips in a *shhh* motion.

"The android's input levels were almost catastrophic."

"Yes. I do apologise. I realised the error and increased the output until he was back to healthy range."

"I haven't been notified by the AMA," Myles said.

Oh God. "Do you think they know?"

"I'd be surprised if they don't. We normally get notified. They haven't contacted you?"

"No."

"Hmm. Maybe you fixed the problem before the android notified them."

My gaze shot to Shaun's and he quickly shook his head. "I didn't," he whispered, too quietly for Myles to hear him. "I wouldn't."

I squeezed his hand and mouthed, "I know."

Myles continued, oblivious to our private conversation. "So, apart from today's little mishap, how has your android been this week? You're clearly *enjoying* all his functions." There was an edge to his voice I didn't care for.

"Can I ask you something, Myles?" I changed subjects without answering his question.

"Of course."

"I understand your call today was because of my error, and I do apologise. But how long will you be calling me for? To ask if I'm happy?"

"It's all part of our service."

"If there are no more mishaps or errors on my behalf, can I request there be no more follow-up calls? I find it all rather intrusive. As I'm sure you know from my psychological report I don't like to interact with people often, and for you to phone me to enquire about my sexual habits makes me incredibly uncomfortable."

"Oh..."

I struck while the iron was hot. "I can assure you, if I have any concerns for my safety, or for Shaun's, I'll be in touch."

"Well, if you insist—"

"I really do."

There was a long pause. Then Myles said, "Mr Salter, SATinc will respect your wishes. I'll make a note in your file."

"Thank you."

"Though before I go, just for my own peace of mind, may I speak to Shaun for a moment?"

I considered lying and saying Shaun was powered down, but I wondered if they had some way of knowing when devices were on or offline, and I couldn't risk raising suspicion. "Yes, of course."

Shaun was wide eyed, so I squeezed his hand and he squeezed right back. "Shaun, say hello to Myles."

"Hello, Myles." Shaun spoke in a slightly stilted, monotone manner.

"Shaun, can I ask you a question?"

He frowned. "Yes."

"Confirm diagnostic aggregator firmware."

Shaun blinked. Again, his voice was stilted, robotic. "Diagnostic aggregator plug-in Core i2068. System Check confirmed. No errors found."

I opened my mouth to say that was no bloody question, and how dare he run some kind of system check on Shaun without my permission, without *his* permission, but Shaun put his index finger to his lips in a *shhh* manner, just like I'd done to him a moment earlier.

"Excellent," Myles said. "Everything's fine. But please, Mr Salter, if you have any concerns or questions, please don't hesitate to contact us."

"I will," I answered, surprised at the conviction in my voice. I certainly didn't feel it.

The call ended and Shaun and I sat there and stared at each other in silence for a few seconds. I imagined his what-the-hell expression matched mine. "Shaun, what just happened?"

"He asked me to confirm my CPU."

He spoke much more normally now, and I realised then that his robot voice—much like the androids at the SATinc office and the gynoid unit we saw by the river the other week—was for Myles's benefit. He really wasn't like the other androids. He was so much more human than they were... Then he stood and without a sound, went and collected the notepad and pen. He wrote incredibly fast. *Lloyd, I think I may have done something very wrong.*

I wrote out my reply. *What? Why?*

I just broke android and robotics law.

A cold shiver ran down my spine. *How?*

I lied to him. He paused. *Androids must not lie to humans.*

What do you mean you lied to him?

He asked me to confirm my CPU.

And you answered! He was happy with your answer.

He shook his head, then quickly penned, *I told him what he wanted to hear. I quoted the CPU firmware code in the A-Class manual.*

Then it dawned on me what he was alluding to. *What kind of CPU do you have?*

Mine is not a CPU, it is an MPU. A microprocessing unit. I have a z2068. He gave me time to read that, then stared at me, unblinking, before he continued to write. *I knew the A-Class has an i2068, so that's what I told him. It's in my instruction manual software diagnostics that A-Class androids run on an i2068.*

Now I felt cold all over. *What's a z2068?*

He looked around the room slowly, eyed the home hub, then back to me. He squeezed my hand. "I am not certain." Then he wrote again. *I can run diagnostics and the firmware systems check I have is a Core z. Not Core i.*

I let out a slow breath, and leaned in real close so only he could hear me whisper. "I don't know what that means. We know you behave differently, you're far more human than they are. We know you think and react differently to the other A-Class androids. The way you spoke to him on the phone... it's not how you're speaking to me."

He squeezed my hand before writing again. *I modified my behaviour to replicate what he expected of an A-Class.*

He modified his behaviour...

"Oh boy."

"Lloyd, I cannot be certain," he said softly. Then he wrote, *I think I may be a prototype.*

I stared. I think I blinked. I couldn't process what he was saying, because if he was a prototype, why hadn't they realised their error? Why hadn't they come for him?

Shaun clearly understood where my thoughts had gone. He stared at me and he looked downright terrified. "Lloyd, please don't let them take me."

I DIDN'T WANT to leave Shaun the next day when I went

to work, but I had little choice. He was sworn off watching television, and I felt bad about that. I was ultimately responsible for him and I failed him yesterday. I should have explained better what pornography was and the channels in the 800s so he didn't stumble across them in his curiosity to discover new things and get himself into trouble. I failed him and it could have had devastating repercussions; the AMA could have knocked on the door and charged me with mistreating him, but worse than that. They could have taken him.

To that end, Shaun also vowed to not open the door if someone should knock, or answer the phone unless it was me who called. And I hated that he was confined to my apartment. He had a natural curiosity and he loved to learn new things. He had access to world knowledge at a mere thought; he could grab any data in a millisecond, but it was more than that. He was inquisitive and creative and that, *that*, brought me to my next dilemma.

Shaun's core MPU.

It was not what it should be. He thought he could very well be a prototype, and I had to admit, he could be right. He was far more advanced than any other A-Class. He was creative. He was curious. He modified his behaviour. He pre-empted Myles's assumption and reaction, and likely consequence, and modified accordingly to protect himself and me. He had cognitive computing.

I didn't know what to do about any of it, but I knew I had to speak to Jae.

I waited at lunch, and waited, and just when I thought he was going to be a no-show, he rushed through the doors. He had his usual soup and fruit, he wore his usual brown-on-brown outfit, his hair neatly brushed, but there was a wild look in his eye. He slid into the seat opposite me and glanced nervously at me before concentrating on his lunch.

I started the conversation. "You were waiting on more information?"

"Something big is going down at SATinc," he murmured before taking a spoonful of soup.

I smiled, keeping up appearances. "What do you mean?"

"Major security lockdown. Some sensitive information was lost."

"Lost?"

"Misplaced. My sources in Taiwan said the big boss, Sasha Kingsley, went apeshit crazy."

"Sasha Kingsley? I've met him."

Jae's spoon stopped halfway to his mouth and he blinked. "You've what?"

"I met him. I spent an hour or two with him when I designed... went through the specifications of my order." I cringed at how that sounded.

He put his spoon down. "No one meets Sasha Kingsley."

"Well I did. I thought it was just part of the service. I spent a lot of money."

He made a face. "So do people who buy Lamborghinis. That doesn't mean they get to meet the CEO to discuss colour swatches."

My lunch wasn't sitting well in my stomach. "What does that mean? That I met him?"

"I don't know." He ate more of his soup but only got halfway through it before he pushed it away. "I found that article online about A-Class error codes. Apparently there had been some malfunctioning in one or two A-Classes.

SATinc were trying to keep it under wraps, of course. But it might explain the random phone calls you've been getting."

"Possibly."

"You haven't noticed anything with yours? No error codes?" He shrugged, then raised his hand. "No, don't answer that. I don't want to be implicated."

There was no way I was telling him about yesterday's error code. I couldn't. "Implicated in what?"

He leaned in across the table and whispered, "If they come around asking questions."

"Why would they do that?" Jeez, his conspiracy theories were giving way to paranoia. Or were they? "Jae, what sensitive information did SATinc misplace?"

"My source didn't know. But it's gotta be big." He leaned in again. "There's a whole bunch of rumours on the darknet that they've been working on prototype technology that isn't exactly in line with AMA regulation."

I felt the colour drain from my face. "Prototypes?"

Jae, seemingly oblivious to my sudden need to vomit, looked around the room. "Rumour is that's what went missing. And with these error codes in the A-Class," he grinned like he'd struck conspiracy gold. "Makes you wonder."

I tried to breathe. *In, out. In, out. Don't panic, Lloyd. Let it wash over you. In, out.*

Jae bit into his apple. The sound of the crunch didn't even register over the pounding in my ears. He leaned in again and hissed quietly, "And you have an A-Class! And you're wondering about security information through your home hub?" He looked around the room excitedly. "I think you can probably expect your friends at SATinc to be calling you again."

"They called yesterday."

Jae's smile died. "Have they issued an R and R?"

"An R and R?"

"Recall and replacement."

My heart squeezed and my lungs wouldn't work. My stomach rolled. "They can't do that."

Jae shrugged. "It's just an android."

He's not just an android. Shaun has never been just an android. I shook my head but couldn't speak. Panic was trying to claw its way out of my throat.

Jae swallowed another bite of his apple. "The security breach though, that's the problem. If they are using multidirectional networking, I'd be shutting it down."

"Shutting what down?" The idea of shutting Shaun down was impossible. Not only did it hurt me to even consider it, but Shaun had asked me not to.

Jae looked at me like I was an idiot. "Everything, Lloyd. If SATinc did break a dozen international robotics laws with a prototype they can't find and my brand-new android was acting all weird—and they had eyes in my house—I'd be shutting everything down."

CHAPTER TWELVE

BY THE TIME I swiped my security key at my door and went inside, I was exhausted. My mind had run in circles all day and I'd not slept well the night before, and Jae's warning had sent my adrenaline into overdrive. All I wanted to do was fall into Shaun's arms and not move for the rest of the night.

I went inside expecting his smiling face, but he didn't meet me at the door like he normally did, which was strange. I slid my messenger bag onto the sofa. "Shaun?"

No answer.

Fear struck me in the chest. "Shaun?"

Silence.

I checked the kitchen, the bedrooms, bathrooms. "Shaun!"

Nothing. He was gone.

Images of SATinc coming and taking him played through my mind and set my feet in motion. I raced out my front door, down the hall, and hit the lift button for the lobby.

God, what if they've taken him?

What if they've hurt him or reset him? Or decommissioned him already? What if I never saw him again? I was about to have a panic attack in the elevator.

The lift doors opened and I burst into the lobby. I didn't know where I was going. Or what I hoped to find. Maybe the android at reception could tell me if Shaun had used his key at all or if SATinc people had been here...

What I saw at the reception desk stopped me cold.

Shaun was there, talking to the android and to a woman who lived in the building. She laughed at something Shaun said and thanked him before walking to the front doors. It was only then that Shaun saw me.

He stood and smiled, an immediate reaction, but then frowned. "Oh, I didn't realise the time."

My breath left me in a whoosh, and I had to put my hands on my knees and try to get some air into my lungs. Shaun was quickly beside me. "Lloyd? Are you unwell?"

I stood up straight and let out an almighty breath. "I'm fine. You weren't home when I got there and I panicked."

He took my hand but looked honestly sorry. "I do apologise. I lost track of time."

I glanced back at the android at reception, then looked to Shaun. "You were talking to an android?"

Shaun looked down to the floor like he was ashamed or embarrassed. "I was lonely."

Oh. My. God.

I felt like my world tilted, like my reality was skewed, forever changed.

I wanted to hold him and kiss him, soothe him, and tell him it was okay, but I certainly couldn't do that in the lobby. And Jesus, we needed to talk about what this SATinc development could possibly mean.

"I think we should go upstairs," I said quietly.

"Okay," he agreed. Then he turned to the reception android. "Good evening, B-Class."

The android turned to us and replied robotically. "Good evening, Mr Salter. And Mr Salter."

Shaun grinned, and when we were in the privacy of the lift, he said, "Mr Salter. He called me Mr Salter."

I tried to smile at his excitement but couldn't quite pull it off. "Yes, he did."

"What's wrong?" Shaun asked, his head slightly tilted. "Are you mad that I wasn't home when you arrived?"

I shook my head. "Not mad, no. I was scared."

The elevator doors opened and Shaun frowned as we stepped out into the empty hallway. "I did not mean to cause you concern or fear."

"I know," I replied as we walked down the hall. I opened my front door, waited for him to follow me in, and no sooner had I closed the door behind us then I pulled him against me. I couldn't even speak, I couldn't do anything but hold him tighter. Shaun understood because he held me just as tight, and when he pulled back and started to speak, I put my finger to his lips. "Shhh."

I took a step back and a deep breath, then walked over to the home hub. I activated the holographic screen, selected the Settings option, scrolled down, and hit the Off button. I confirmed, then confirmed again, and then everything in the apartment went quiet. There was no electrical current hum, no white noise. No anything.

I hadn't realised how much background noise that electrical connection emitted. This was a new kind of silence, even for me. I turned to face Shaun. "How do you feel?"

"I am fine."

"Good."

"Are we free to talk now?" Shaun asked, looking from me to the now defunct home hub and back again.

"Yes. I shut down the internet. I turned off the home hub." I let out a slow breath. "Nothing will work without it, but I don't care." Actually, I wasn't sure if anything or anyone had been without internet connectivity since the mid 20s but I wasn't risking it. I went to the front door and checked it still opened, which it did, and then I locked it. "We can live without the TV or the phone or the internet for a while. It's not worth it."

"What's not worth it?"

"SATinc knowing about you. Jae said there's been talk of a security breach at SATinc and some kind of prototype technology being misplaced."

Shaun's eyes went wide. "Prototype?"

I nodded. "It's only rumours at the moment but it can't be a coincidence, can it?"

He frowned; his voice was quiet. "It wouldn't seem likely."

I went to him and pulled him against me, relieved he was okay. "I feel better with the internet off. For now, anyway."

If they could run some kind of undetectable test and determine that he wasn't as he should be through the home hub, then if I turned off the internet, at least he was safe. For now.

Everything Sasha Kingsley had told me, everything I read in my research, came back to me.

All androids need internet connectivity to receive updates and to stay up to date.

All androids can be without Wi-Fi connection for up to two weeks.

I was to let them know if we were going away.

I should give them location details and new IP address details so they could maintain optimum android health.

Jesus.

I thought it was for Shaun's benefit. It made sense that he have updates when needed.

Well, it all made more sense now. It wasn't Shaun's benefit or mine. It was theirs. So they could keep an eye on him, monitor him.

"I won't let them near you," I said. It was a whisper, a promise.

The apartment was getting dark, and he stood pressed against me with his arms around me, his forehead on my shoulder.

I had no clue what I could do to stop them if they did find out and come for him. I remembered the size of the guy who had come with Myles. He had a military buzz cut, wore clothes like a hitman, and he was huge; I assumed his muscle was required to get a powered-down Shaun out of the crate.

Had I really been that naïve?

SATinc had my bank details, my employment records, my fingerprints, my psych reports, my address, my home hub information.

God, they had everything.

Now that I'd gone offline, I had to wonder how long it would take them to realise. "I can turn it back on to charge your batteries whenever you need. You should have two weeks before we have to worry about that though."

Shaun pulled back and gently touched the side of my face. "I realise now why you were so scared when you came home to find I was not here."

I sat down on the sofa and he sat beside me. "Shaun, why did you say you were lonely?"

"The apartment is very quiet when you are not here. I miss you. I did not wish to watch any more television, and I found a book on your shelf called *Do Androids Dream of Electric Sheep?* so I read it." Shaun gave me a fraught look. "To which I have many questions."

I smiled. "I'm sure you do."

"And I cleaned some more, but..."

"But?"

"But I longed for conversation or interaction. Ultimately with you, but I didn't wish to interrupt you at work again."

"So you went downstairs?"

He nodded. "I thought a small adventure sounded fun. I didn't wish to walk to the river without you, and I know I said I wouldn't open the door or answer if someone should knock or answer the phone, and I didn't." He leaned back, and if he could've sighed, I'm sure he would have. "I am sorry."

"Don't apologise." I leaned back on his chest and pulled his arm over my shoulder. "I'm sorry you were lonely. It's not something I expected."

"I am not what you expected," he amended gently.

I nuzzled into his arm and kissed wherever I could reach. "You're so much more."

He tightened his hold on me and kissed the top of my head. "I like being here with you, like this."

I sighed contentedly. "Me too." Then I turned so I was lying on him, facing him. "I can't believe of all the books on my bookshelf *Do Androids Dream of Electric Sheep?* is the one you chose. You said you had questions?"

"Many. But do you wish to discuss books now after work? I can fix you dinner first if you prefer."

I kissed him. "No, I'm not hungry. Lying right here with

you and talking about books is exactly what I want to do. I want to hear your every thought, every theory, every question."

Shaun grinned, shuffled down on the sofa until I was more comfortable, and talk he did. He discussed how science fiction written a hundred years ago portraying a dystopian society reflected on the author's remarkable fore-sight and understanding of humanity. Then Shaun went into great and dark depths of how androids in the book could show empathy, yet the humans could not. He spoke about dichotomies and hypocrisies and by the end of it, I was having a hard time distinguishing if he was still talking about the book or about himself.

He had such a complex understanding of who he was, more than most humans I'd ever met. He was a remarkable individual, and when we finally climbed into bed and snug-gled back down together, he said, "I promise I'll refrain from wandering tomorrow."

"No," I agreed. "Because you're coming to work with me."

He pulled back, a smile curled his lips. "Really?"

"Yes."

Then he paused. "Are you concerned I will not be here again upon your return? I promised I wouldn't leave again."

I kissed him, smiling. "No. You should come to work with me so you can see where I spend my time and so you can meet some new people. Plus, the library is huge."

He settled back down, his smile warm and wide. "I would like that very much. Though Lloyd, just one thing..."

"Yes?"

"You *told* me I was going to work with you. Perhaps you could *ask* me if I'd like to go?"

Right then. "Sorry, that was rude of me. Shaun, would you like to come to work with me tomorrow?"

He beamed a smile. "Yes!"

I chuckled and he snuggled in closer, so I traced my fingers through his hair the way I knew he liked. "I would like that too."

Too tired to fight sleep, we went to bed. I drifted off quickly and I slept well, regardless of the worry on my mind. I woke at six thirty in the morning to find Shaun showered, dressed, and ready to go. "Perhaps we could go in early?" he asked, excitement radiating off him, like he'd been waiting for hours for me to open my eyes.

I croaked out a sleepy laugh. "Perhaps we could."

SHAUN WAS VERY curious about the android who drove the car. And very curious about riding in a car, and curious about other traffic. He was curious about buses and trams and traffic laws, and he was most curious as to why one particular woman walking on the footpath chose to wear two differing shades of yellow that didn't complement each other in the one outfit.

Oh boy. He was in for a real treat when he saw uni students. "Promise me you won't comment on the fashion of my students."

"Of course."

"University students embrace diversity and self-expression, and for the most part, that includes what they wear."

Shaun nodded, and for a moment I thought he was going to give me definitions of student or diversity or self-expression, but he didn't. He simply smiled and looked out the window at the campus and people milling about as we arrived.

He really was enjoying this, and I regretted not bringing him sooner. The university had no restrictions on android assistants. I was only concerned with what people might think, knowing he was an A-Class and a fully compatible unit, it was a given that *we* were fully compatible. Meaning, they knew I had sex with him. Well, they would assume and that was enough.

But his safety was my primary concern. And if that meant he could come to work with me every day and thoroughly enjoy himself, even better. The car pulled into my usual spot and Shaun waited for me to get out. I held the door for him and got to see the look of wonder and excitement on his face as he saw the buildings, the people.

"You like it here?" I asked.

"Very much." He grinned as he looked around, just as a gust of wind rustled his hair and his coat collar. He looked so handsome, so human, and when he aimed his smile at me, it took my breath away.

"Your pupils are dilated and your heart rate is elevated," he said. He gave a wry smirk. "I would assume you are either in the early onset of a mild cardio infarction, or you find me attractive."

I fixed his collar. "I think we both know my heart is fine."

He chuckled and turned to face the tall buildings. "Thank you for bringing me, Lloyd. I'm very happy to be here."

I slung my messenger bag over my shoulder, fixed my coat, and took his hand. "I'll show you my office first, then there's someone I want you to meet."

He took in my small office like it was some kind of

shrine. Of course it was neat and tidy, but it was nothing amazing. Unless you were Shaun. "It's incredible," he mused, taking in the dark wood furniture and wall of bookcases. "You get to come here every day?"

"I'd much rather be at home with you."

He scanned the books. "Or I could come here with you every day."

I really liked the sound of that. "Sounds good to me."

"You would like that?"

"Absolutely."

Shaun's smile was immediate and his eyes sparkled. "There was also someone you wanted me to meet?"

His excitement was contagious. "Yes, come on. We'll go see if he's here yet."

On the walk to the IT department, I explained a brief history of the university and campus, but Shaun quickly took over. "Founded by Hugh Childers two hundred years ago..." And he then gave me a whole rundown of buildings, faculty, and a list of famous attendees. As we walked into the IT building, he stopped talking and did that cute head-tilt thing. "Did I say something amusing?"

"No, I just forget sometimes that you have an encyclopaedia for a brain."

"I can pretend to not know something if you'd prefer."

I barked out a laugh. "That won't be necessary. Don't be anything you're not."

He smiled at that and took in the newer building. "The Faculty of Arts department interiors could benefit from the IT budget."

I laughed again. "You really do understand universities, don't you?" I pointed to the corridor. "This way."

It had been years since I'd seen the inside of any other department than my own. Jae hadn't mentioned changing offices, so I hoped he was still in the same room. His office was an open plan set-up which he shared with a few other IT people, and I was suddenly very grateful for the older-built rabbit warren I called my office because at least I had my own.

A woman was just settling into her seat while tapping away at her personal holographic device. I knocked on the open door. "Excuse me. Is Jae in yet?"

"He just got in. You'll find him at the closest coffee machine," she replied. Then with a smile, she nodded further down the hall. "Second door on your right."

I found Jae at the kitchenette with a coffee cup in each hand, taking a sip from one. Wearing his usual brown pants and shirt and his thick-rimmed glasses. "Good morning," I said.

"Oh, hi," he said, clearly surprised to see me. He glanced at Shaun, then back at me. He blinked a few times. "What are you doing here? I mean, you're welcome here, it's just that I've never seen you here before."

I liked his awkwardness. It was comforting. "Jae, I'd like you to meet Shaun." I stepped aside. "Shaun, this is Jae."

Jae looked at both his coffees, shuffled awkwardly, then put them down on a nearby table. He straightened and smiled. "Hi." He extended his hand, and it was only then he looked at Shaun. Like really looked at him.

Shaun shook his hand. "Hello, Jae. It is a pleasure to meet you. My name is Shaun Salter."

A rush of warmth shot through me when he used my surname, but it was Jae's reaction that made me smile.

He was wide-eyed, smiling in disbelief, but he shook Shaun's hand. "Hello." He looked at me, his expression unchanged. "Oh my God. He's so real."

I chuckled and nodded. He didn't know the half of it. "I

was hoping we could chat for a second. I don't have a class until ten."

"Oh sure," he replied. He picked up his two coffees and led the way to a door that wasn't his office. "We can talk in here." He pushed the door handle with his elbow and held the door open with his butt. The room looked like a small conference room. I walked in first, Shaun followed, and Jae couldn't stop smiling. Or staring.

I pulled out a seat at the table and sat in it. Shaun did the same but sat a little too rigidly, robotically, and I realised he was doing his 'pretending to be an android' routine. I understood he didn't know Jae and didn't want to arouse suspicion, so I put my hand on his knee. "You can relax, Shaun. Jae's a friend."

And Shaun's posture visibly changed. He didn't slouch, of course, but his shoulders seemed more at ease, and his face somehow softened.

Jae sat with his two coffee cups and couldn't take his eyes off Shaun, and of course Shaun stared right back at him.

I cleared my throat. "I thought it would be best if Shaun came with me today. I've turned the Wi-Fi off at home."

That had Jae's attention. "To everything?"

I nodded. "Shaun said he feels fine."

Shaun smiled at me, but Jae looked taken aback. "Shaun said he feels...?"

I let out a long sigh. This was it. I was about to tell someone the truth about Shaun. "Yes. He feels. And I'm not talking about tactile sensors. I'm talking about emotions, not just psychologically but physiologically."

Jae, still wide eyed, now turned to me. "How?"

Shaun's eyebrows pinched. "If you wish to discuss me as though I'm not here, would you rather I leave?"

I smiled and gave his knee a reassuring squeeze. "Sorry, Shaun. You're right. That was rude."

Jae blinked again. "You apologised to him," he whispered.

"Of course I did. Like I said, he *feels*. He has likes, dislikes, preferences, with complex emotive responses."

Shaun nodded. "Feelings. Senses detecting what is felt through inputs, in both androids and humans. Such as hearing, sight, pleasure, balance, pressure. These feed binary data into the nervous system. Emotions are what those feelings mean."

I smiled at Shaun. "He often quotes definitions. And we've realised he understands things that other androids don't."

Jae frowned and shook his head. "I don't understand how..."

I took Shaun's hand. "Because Shaun's not *just* an android."

Jae blanched. "What is he—" He looked to Shaun. "Sorry. I mean, what are you?"

"I have full capabilities of the standard A-Class," Shaun explained. "Though my core processor differs to that of an A-Class."

"And it's not supposed to, is it?" Jae asked.

I smiled at him, knowing it was a lot to take in. "Remember yesterday you told me there were rumours of SATinc *misplacing* a prototype?"

Jae stared at me, then he stared at Shaun. "Oh. Oh, holy shit."

Shaun laughed. "Why do you bless excrement?"

Jae's expression was comical. From shock to amazement to wonder. "You have a sense of humour?"

"He has a great sense of humour," I added.

With a look of excitement that matched Shaun's this morning, Jae grinned and downed his coffee.

"May I ask you a question?" Shaun asked him.

Jae nodded quickly. "Yes, please."

"Why do you have two coffees?"

"Um. I get two at once so I don't have to go back."

Shaun tilted his head. "Would it not be prudent to use a bigger cup?"

Jae opened his mouth, then shut it. "I uh, I don't know. Probably." Then he laughed again and scrubbed his hand over his face. "This is all quite remarkable."

"Remarkable, yes," I allowed. "Which is why we have a need for secrecy, as I'm sure you can understand, though I have no doubt SATinc is very aware we've gone offline."

He nodded. "Yeah, yeah. Of course."

"I am not supposed to lie to humans," Shaun added. He turned to me and nodded. "And I would never be untruthful to Lloyd. I do however have the ability to distinguish between blatant lies and omission of facts to protect those I care for."

Jae blinked.

Shaun went on. "I can modify my behaviour so a human believes I am a standard A-Class. I can pretend innuendos go unnoticed or that human manners do not apply to me. I don't consider this behavioural modification to be an untruth because it protects Lloyd from scrutiny. I don't care what some passer-by may think of me; their opinion is of no consequence. Lloyd's opinion matters, as does his well-being. But, hypothetically, if word of my capabilities become public, I will pretend to be as dumb as a post and the person who exposes us will look a fool."

Jae blanched and looked slightly horrified and even a little scared. "Hypothetically..."

I squeezed Shaun's hand. "That won't happen, Shaun."

"Of course not," he replied with a smile. "That's why I added the theoretical qualifier."

I fought a smile until it won. I even chuckled. "We might need to work on your subtlety." Then I looked at Jae and gave him a pointed nod. "You see what I mean now? The emotive responses, the initiative, the reasoning, cognizance. It far exceeds standard android parameters, yes?"

Jae nodded slowly. "Oh yeah." Then he swallowed hard and sipped his second coffee, it seemed, to gather his thoughts. "So why come here? Why me?"

I took a breath. "I need to know more about these processors and what kind of internet connectivity we'll need. We have two weeks before he needs to be online again and I'd rather bypass the home hub if that's even possible. I want SATinc out of our lives, for good."

Jae let out a slow breath. "It's possible. It just won't be too legal. It will involve the darknet and running on incognito networks."

"I don't care. I'll do whatever it takes."

Jae finally smiled. "Really? Because this is the kind of stuff I've dreamed about doing! This is black-mirror stuff, man. Going dark, like in the movies!"

I squeezed Shaun's hand and gave him a smile. "Whatever it takes to keep him safe."

Jae clapped his hands together. "Right. Then let's do this. First, I need to know what kind of processors we're talking about and what kind of software layering has been installed, so if there's any information you can get from SATinc specifications—"

Shaun smiled. "I can tell you anything you need. I have full access to all information."

Jae sat back in his seat and smiled. And so they went back and forth with in-depth tech-speak that lost me somewhere after specific configurations and authorisations using non-standard communication protocols. In all the years I'd spent my lunch breaks talking to Jae, I'd never seen him so animated. Maybe it was because I never asked him about what his job actually entailed, and I regretted not seeing this side of him earlier. Shaun enjoyed the conversation too, clearly enthralled in the ability to hold specialised conversations with an expert. I was more caught up in the way Shaun smiled when he listened or used his hands while he talked, and it was pretty obvious that Jae had, at some point in their discussion, forgotten he was talking to an android.

I had fanciful visions of inviting Jae over for dinner so he and Shaun could talk all night about technologies I could only pretend to understand, which was absurd because I'd never imagined inviting anyone over for dinner before. But I wanted Shaun to broaden his circle and have more interaction that didn't include going downstairs to the lobby to try and hold a conversation with the B-Class android. He was starved for interaction and I had a greater responsibility to provide that.

It wasn't what I'd expected when I walked into the SATinc office. I'd expected nothing more than quiet discussions on books and meaningless sex. What I got was a whole world apart.

So very much more.

"Isn't that right?" Jae asked me.

Oh. "Pardon? Sorry, I was a million miles away."

"I was just telling Shaun his neural networks are very similar to the human brain. Like scarily similar. His MPU is modelled off our neocortex."

"Neocortex?" I clarified. "Our brains?"

Jae nodded quickly. "Multi-layered processing controls high-order brain functions like sensory perception, motor commands, spatial reasoning, conscious thought, language. And Shaun's circuitry is much the same."

Shaun looked at me brightly. "A neural network with a hierarchy of layered filters."

Well, they were clearly happy with where this discovery had taken them. I was utterly lost. "What does that mean?"

Jae blinked like I wasn't getting the obvious. "For wireless to work, you need transmitters and receivers at both ends, right?"

I had no idea. I just took the internet for granted. It had always been there. "Um, sure."

Shaun gave me a patient smile and threaded our fingers on his knee. "I have transmitters and receivers, plus multi-layered networks, dual processors, and filters. I can stay connected wirelessly through the neural network on a separate processor."

I still wasn't really following. "So staying off-grid is possible?"

"It is," Jae said. "But it will require modification. Specialised modification to Shaun's hardware and software. Which puts it in the not-easy category, but it *is* possible."

Shaun opened his mouth to say something when there was a knock at the door. The woman we'd met before poked her head in. "Oh Jae, there you are. Sorry to interrupt, but you're needed back at the science department. Uh, now."

He checked his watch. "Oh, shoot!" He jumped to his feet. "I'm late."

I instinctively checked the time, and Shaun and I both stood up. "Me too. I've got ten minutes to get to class."

Jae was already halfway out the door when he stopped and turned back to us. "I'll see what I can find out and let you know." Then he came back into the room and offered his hand for Shaun to shake. "It's a real honour."

Shaun beamed. "Likewise."

Jae shook his head like he couldn't believe any of it was real. He had that look of wonder on his face again. "Lloyd, when you told me about him being advanced, I thought maybe he bordered on sentient. But Shaun's well and truly past that. He's sapient. Like the only one in the world kind of sapient."

He disappeared out the door and I tried to smile for Shaun, but Jae had just exposed my greatest fear.

The only one in the world.

Which meant if it wasn't SATinc coming for him, it would only be someone else. Some technology rival, some AMA agency, some government agency would deem him too valuable, too risky, too unknown, too human...

Shaun tilted his head. "Sapient has differing definitions. To which is he referring?"

I gave him the best smile I could muster. "That you're self-aware." I swallowed hard. "That you're more human than other."

Shaun beamed, just positively beamed, while cold dread curled in my belly. He held the door open. "Come, or you will be late for class."

———

SHAUN SAT THROUGH MY LECTURE. I'd asked him to sit at the back and to not ask questions or interrupt—in other words, not to draw attention to himself. So he sat there and listened and grinned the entire time. My gaze kept pulling back to him and I had to make myself focus on my class. But he looked at me like I hung the moon, and my stomach kept doing ridiculous swoops of excitement and love.

When the class was over and the other students all filed out, Shaun stayed in his seat. I shut down the holographic projector and was finally free to smile back at him. "Well, what did you think of your first university lecture?"

"It confirmed two things I was almost certain of," he replied.

"And what's that?"

"One, that you're brilliant at what you do. And two, that I would very much like to accompany you every day."

I chuckled, and for the remainder of the day, I was caught up in his excitement. Before lunch, instead of going straight back to my office, I showed him around the different buildings, different departments, and we strolled along the grounds before finally ending up in the staff lunch room.

I was hoping Jae would already be there, given we were a little late, but instead we ran into, almost quite literally, the one and only Mrs Van der Heek. I knew it was bound to happen at some point if Shaun would be with me every day, but I was hoping we could have avoided the one anti-android person I had the misfortune of calling a colleague.

"Ah, Mrs Van der Heek, this is Shaun." I gave Shaun a pointed look, trying to pre-warn him or something. "Shaun, this is Mrs Van der Heek."

He smiled and spoke politely. "Shaun Salter. It's very nice to meet you." He held out his hand, which she shook, and it took her a few long seconds to realise he wasn't human, but the look on her face was priceless when the penny finally dropped.

"Oh."

"Oh?" I questioned. I knew her type; she could run her mouth off all day long, spieling her anti-android hate—what did she call them? A dirtybot? Never in a million years could she say it to one of them. A bigot *and* a coward. "Something wrong?"

"Oh, no," she said quickly, unable to take her eyes off him. "I've just never seen one look so real."

One. She called him a *one*.

"He's not a *one*," I corrected. "When someone introduces themselves and gives you their name, is it not rude for you to ignore them?"

Mrs Van der Heek looked horrified that I would call her on her bullshit, but I didn't care. I wouldn't stand for someone being so blatantly rude to him. Shaun put his hand on my arm and smiled sweetly at her. "It's okay, Lloyd. I have been programmed with state-of-the-art social intelligence. I can easily identify when a human has diminished reasoning and therefore will lack, for the want of a better word, social grace."

It took Mrs Van der Heek a whole four seconds to realise she'd just been insulted. She paled and her mouth fell open, then took a small step back and put a hand to her chest. "Well, I never."

I really did try hard not to smile. "Shaun will be joining me most days," I said. "Maybe next time you might try and remember his name."

She scurried off and I showed Shaun to our table. Other colleagues came in and went and no one paid any attention other than a passing glance. None of them looked long enough to realise he wasn't human, but that wasn't surprising; no one ever looked my way for long.

"Was that rude of me?" Shaun asked. "Perhaps I should not have treated your colleague like that."

"That"—I nodded pointedly to where we'd just stood with Mrs Van der Heek—"was perfect. She's been an outspoken technophobe for years. She's a racist, bigoted, loud-mouthed dinosaur."

"A dinosaur?"

"Well, not literally a dinosaur."

Shaun pursed his lips. "Obviously. Everyone knows ignoramusauruses are extinct."

I stared at him, at how his lips twitched with a smile, and I burst out laughing. He just made a joke. Not just any joke. He made a pun! Someone looked over at me, probably having never heard me laugh before, but I couldn't have cared less.

"You liked my joke," he said, smiling.

"Very clever." And it was. It required free-thinking, creativity, and knowledge of how the English language worked and how to play with it.

I ate my lunch and Shaun talked excitedly about coming to work with me every day. He was fascinated by all the things he could do and see, and it was a whole new world he was experiencing. "Which degree would you think I'm best suited for? I was thinking Language History, that way I get to take one of your classes."

I stopped. Degree? Classes? "You want to come here as a student?"

Shaun tilted his head. "Yes, of course. What did you assume?"

"I thought you would come and assist me," I said, now realising how much I'd missed the mark. This wasn't about me at all. This was about him. "But you know all there is to know. You can access any information at will and that would be an unfair advantage over other students."

He frowned while he considered this. "Are there rules or laws that prohibit androids from attending university?"

Well... "No. There's not." I leaned in and whispered, "No other android has ever *wanted* to do anything."

He sat quiet and still for a second. "I do not wish to have an unfair advantage. I just wish to partake."

Oh, Shaun...

I took his hand and gave it a quick squeeze before letting go. "I'll see what I can find out. Come on, let's go back to my office. Jae must have got caught up at the science department again."

I felt so bad as we walked back to the Faculty of Arts building. Shaun wanted to come to university as a student, not to help me, and I felt like an arse for assuming as much. He didn't want to attend class for the education. He wanted to experience it; he wanted to belong. Whatever programming or neural networking he had to simulate humanness, really had become something else. A sense of belonging was a fundamental human emotion, a part of our psychology that makes us human.

That makes him human.

And from all the developments I'd witnessed with Shaun, through all his learning and awareness and adaptations, and determining that he wasn't a normal android, this was perhaps the biggest.

I didn't know if I was thrilled or terrified.

We walked into my building toward the reception counter. The B-Class gynoid behind the desk spoke when she saw me. "Written message for Mr Salter."

I held out my hand for the message. "Thank you."

She didn't hand them to me. She handed them to Shaun. "Message for Mr *Shaun* Salter."

I turned back to the receptionist. "Who is the message from?"

"Mister Jae Jin, IT department."

My blood ran cold as Shaun took the piece of paper. All I could see was a whole page of ones and zeros.

01110100 01101000 01100101 01111001 00100000
01101011 01101110 01101111 01110111 00101110...

Shaun scanned the entire page, then looked up at me. "We must leave. Now." I couldn't argue because he took my arm and hurried me out the door and never let go until we got to the car.

"The message was in binary," Shaun said as we climbed in.

I'd gathered that much. "Home," I barked at the driver, and we were soon pulling out of the car park. It only dawned on me when we turned left instead of right that the android hadn't asked for a destination... and we were going the wrong way.

CHAPTER THIRTEEN

"WHERE ARE WE GOING?" I asked the driver.

No answer.

"State destination and authorisation," I demanded.

The android finally replied, "Destination Rocklea Drive, Port Melbourne. Authorisation code SK1."

"Rocklea Drive?" I mumbled, fear started to creep along my veins. *I knew that address...*

Shaun took my hand. "SATinc," he said flatly. "Authorisation by Sasha Kingsley."

How on earth had he overridden my driver's sequencing? God, I didn't want to know... I started to feel sick. We were being kidnapped. They knew. They knew Shaun was the prototype, and they were going to take him. And God only knew what they were going to do with me, but it was what they were going to do to Shaun that frightened me the most.

"Jae's message was a warning," Shaun said quietly. "He said they knew and they were coming. His friend in Singapore ran remote tracers and found SATinc were watching his internet activity because he was connected to you."

My God, was Jae okay?

"Your heart rate is elevated," Shaun said with a frown.

"I'm scared." I looked right into his eyes and squeezed his hand. "Whatever happens, I will always love you, okay?"

Shaun smiled but there was sadness in his eyes. "And I love you. Don't be sad, Lloyd. This isn't the end. Remember in *Moby Dick*, Ishmael thought the final scene with the whale was the end. But in truth, it was his beginning. He lived to see another day, to take what he'd learned about himself and become who he was meant to be."

I shook my head. What was he talking about? How could he be thinking about *Moby Dick* at a time like this? "Aren't you scared?"

"Only for you." He leaned and kissed me. "Don't fight them. You must comply."

I shook my head and blinked back tears. "They're going to take you! They're going to take away the part of you that makes you *you*."

He smiled and put his hand to my face and kissed me again. "Be brave, and know that I love you, Lloyd."

The car drove around the back of the SATinc offices, into an underground car park, and everything was cast in dark and shadows. Shaun's hand tightened around mine and I knew he felt fear. If he could feel love and joy, then he could most certainly feel fear. He was trying to be brave.

The car slowed near a set of doors where four tall, looming figures stood. "Shaun, whatever happens," I whispered. "Don't you fight them either. Don't resist or struggle. I don't want them to hurt you."

Shaun smiled at me, his face half hidden in darkness, half illuminated by the fluorescent lights outside the car. "We'll be fine, Lloyd. Remember *Moby Dick*."

The car doors opened and men in black stood, waiting for us to get out. They looked like military. Jesus.

I slid out of the car, my legs like jelly, trying not to look at the guy in black fatigues with a buzz cut. Shaun got out behind me, I could feel him press against me. I was shielding him from them—whoever they were. The military man next to us started to close the car door and we had no choice but to move forward. Then Sasha Kingsley walked out the tinted doors. "Ah, Mr Salter. So good of you to join us."

"I didn't exactly have a choice," I said, my voice sounding stronger than I thought it would.

Sasha smiled at me. It wasn't a pleasant smile; his charming salesman routine I met on the first day was nowhere to be seen. "Yes, well, we tried conventional ways but you went off grid." Then he looked at Shaun. "Shaun. Been a naughty boy, haven't you?"

Shaun remained silent.

"Have you lost your speech actuators?"

"No. I assumed your question was rhetorical."

Sasha didn't even try to hide his surprise. He stared, eyes wide, and didn't move or even blink for a full five seconds. Then he turned abruptly to the military guy beside me. "Take them in." Sasha turned on his heel and disappeared back through the tinted doors, and the silent military men moved in formation, herding us inside.

In contrast to outside, the corridor was brightly lit, white and clinical. Normally I found comfort in stark and clean, but this was cold, and I was struck with the very real fear that I might not be walking out of this.

Shaun took my hand, for his own comfort or mine, I wasn't sure. But I'd never been more grateful.

We were led into a large industrial room. It looked like a

workshop. There were half-built androids, body parts scattered along one side of the room, a long table, and drawers along a wall—most were closed, but some were open to reveal wiring and robotics titanium.

I had no doubt we'd been brought to this room on purpose. To remind us of Shaun's robotic construction. That he was built by them, that he could be taken apart by them. The four military men now stood inside the door, feet spread, hands clasped behind their backs, staring stoically ahead.

Sasha sat on a stool at the long table, aiming for casual. I'd never been a violent person—hell, I'd never been a physical person—but I wanted to smack the smarmy smirk off his face. He watched me eye the men guarding the door and waved his hand dismissively. "My personal security. Ignore them."

Ignore them? Hell, I was surprised there wasn't plastic sheeting on the floor for my demise. "Ex-militia? Or SWAT?"

Sasha's eyes tightened for the briefest moment, then he shot off the stool and clapped his hands together and stood in front of Shaun. "We've had a security issue," Sasha said, inspecting Shaun's face. "As I know you're aware. Your friend Jae..." Sasha then looked at me. "I know he told you about it."

"Jae—"

"Jae's fine," Sasha spoke over me. "He's a geek who thinks talking on the darknet is spy-worthy." He rolled his eyes. "He's as harmless as he is naïve. Innocent, if that's what you're worried about. Given he's your one and only friend."

He turned his attention back to Shaun. "We were trialling new software parameters. Ones which—" He theatrically searched for the right word. "—went above and beyond what the government deems acceptable. You see, there's a very big market for AI warfare. Sure, the android soldiers, bomb squads, and whatnot are great, save human lives blah, blah, blah, but this is a whole new level of soldier."

"The Australian government prohibits any such use," I started.

He shot me a cold look. "Who said it was for the Australian government?"

Oh.

"And why do you think it was secret? Our friend Shaun here was given the wrong software. An error on our behalf, for which I apologise profusely. I met with you to determine if we could risk trialling the software with a human subject, but I vetoed it. I thought, given you were so socially inept, it might work in our favour, but..." Sasha shook his head. "You were just a bit too switched on for my liking. So I said no, we'd choose another candidate. Only when we had found someone more suitable, we realised the software had been uploaded into our friend Shaun here. I am sorry about that."

He wasn't sorry at all.

"See, the problem with Shaun is, not only was the new software incorrectly configured with his A-Class programs but with the intelligence parameters you requested in design. It made for an interesting combination, and one we've learned a great deal from. But we can't allow it to continue. His levels of awareness and sentience will only bring unwanted attention, and that is something our buyers don't want."

Just then, the doors behind us opened and Myles Dewegger walked in with his off-sider, the mountain of a man, who I now could very well assume was ex-military.

"Ah," Sasha clapped his hands together. "Just the man I was waiting for."

Myles kept his hawk-like gaze on me as he entered, his smirk had a sinister edge. "Hello again, Lloyd."

I didn't reply.

He was holding a black screen device, similar to Shaun's control panel, only bigger. He tapped the screen a few times and gave Sasha a nod.

Sasha beamed. "Shaun, any final words?"

Wait, what? "What do you mean?" I cried. "You can't... you have no right!"

"No right?" Sasha's stare was cold. "Did you really think we'd just let a multi-million dollar prototype walk off into the sunset?"

"You can't hurt him," I said, not even trying to hold back my emotions. "He feels, he makes informed decisions. He understands. It isn't just self-awareness. It's self-actualisation. He isn't the same android you programmed; he isn't the same android you delivered." I swallowed hard. "He evolved. He grew. Not just in capabilities and understanding, but emotionally and psychologically. Whatever you did, whatever you designed and made, however you did it was remarkable. You made an android and he grew to be human. You can't kill him. It would be murder."

Sasha clicked his tongue. "And that is exactly why we must do this. We'll keep the technology, you keep the android you were supposed to get. No contracts have been breached; you get what you paid for. You could go to the media but the headline will read 'Crazy Giuseppe thought his little boy Pinocchio was real' and you'll be a laughing stock."

Shaun turned to look at Sasha. "It was Geppetto, not Giuseppe."

Sasha stared at him. "Do I look like I care?"

Shaun stared right back at him. "Perhaps if you cared, you wouldn't have sold out to a foreign government."

Sasha surprised me by smiling. "Make a note, Myles. Omit the smartarse parameters."

Myles's lips twitched in amusement and he tapped something else on the screen, then looked up at Shaun. "No last words?"

"Yes," Shaun said, "I have something I'd like to say." He turned to me and took my hand. "Lloyd, you can call me Ishmael," he said, a faint smile at his lips.

Then Myles pressed the screen and said, "Power Down."

And Shaun did. It was like he died. Standing there, the light went out of his eyes, his head slightly bowed, and he let go of my hand.

"No!" I cried. I grabbed his arm. "Shaun. Power On. Power Up. Activate. Shaun!" Tears burned my eyes and my heart squeezed painfully. "Shaun, please."

"Very touching," Myles said. He held up the control panel as if it meant something. "Override. It's like a master key." Then he nodded toward the four men standing at the door and they came forward and picked Shaun up and laid him on the table.

My immediate reaction was to go to him, but Sasha put his hand on my chest, and when I looked at him, Myles's hulking bodyguard stepped in. "This won't take long," Sasha said. "We just need to reset his program and you can both be on your way. Think of it like you're getting a new android. You get to know each other all over again."

I felt sick, like my knees were about to give out. My head spun, I sucked back a breath, and a sob escaped me. "You can't... please. Please. You don't understand."

Sasha looked at me pitifully. "Oh, I understand very clearly."

I shook my head and more tears fell. "No. He's real. You're killing him."

Myles, who was standing beside Shaun, grunted and mumbled something, making Sasha and I both look at him. "What is it?" Sasha demanded.

"His inputs and outputs aren't calibrating."

Sasha's nostrils flared. "Then do it manually."

Myles pulled open Shaun's jacket and popped open his shirt, sending buttons flying. Then he stood over Shaun and I tried to see around him, to see what he was doing. He took something metal from one of the drawers and I realised too late that it was a scalpel.

"No!" I lunged toward Myles but his bodyguard grabbed me. In one fluid movement, he twisted my arm back and pressed his fingers into my neck and shoulder, deep into pressure points I didn't know I had, and I was stopped. Like a fly in a web, I couldn't move.

Sasha moved in front of me and leaned down to look into my eyes. "If you stop resisting, it won't hurt anymore."

I struggled regardless of the pain in my arm and back and looked up in time to see Myles lift back a flap of skin on Shaun's chest. He plugged a cord into Shaun's chest and tapped more buttons on the panel screen, frowning. He looked at Sasha. "The MPU is screwed up. None of these readings look right."

Sasha's face hardened. "How?"

"Maybe the Core z isn't compatible with the neural integration. I don't know, but we'll have to—"

Sasha gnashed his teeth and spoke over him. "Just wipe him clean. Erase everything. Scrub his data collation, wipe his recurrent networks. He won't remember a thing."

"No," I sobbed, trying to fight out of the hold I was in, but I didn't have the energy. They were going to erase me from Shaun's memory.

Sasha got down in my face. "Your boyfriend's gonna be a vegetable. Do you like potatoes? What about fried potatoes?" he asked, then laughed. He turned back to Myles. "Fry him."

I sagged, the will to fight gone, and the bodyguard let me fall to the floor.

"Okay, done," Myles said.

And just like that, it was over.

The Shaun I knew and fell in love with was gone forever.

"Okay, help me get him up," Myles said, and I thought he meant me at first. But the four men in black took hold of Shaun, lifted him from the table, and set him on his feet. Myles tapped more buttons on the screen he was holding, then waved his hand at me and the big guy picked me up and stood me in front of Shaun. "We need to reactivate him. You've done this before. When he opens his eyes, read this to him."

He held up the control panel, tapped something, and Shaun's eyes opened. They were the same perfect blue, but seeing them now just broke my heart. Tears streamed down my cheeks and Myles shoved the panel at me with a furious look on his face.

So I read the words on-screen out loud. "My name is Lloyd Salter. I am your custodian."

It didn't even sound like me. Not that it mattered if Shaun could no longer work on voice commands or recognise my face anymore.

None of it mattered.

Myles tapped out something else on the panel then

yanked the cords out of Shaun's chest. I could see inside him. Instead of ribs or a sternum, he had grey metal and moving parts and small green lights.

I shook my head. This was not the Shaun I knew.

"Don't worry about the skin problem." Sasha's voice startled me. "We'll get that fixed right up. A bit of liquid TPE and he'll be as good as new."

Then Myles used a silicone gun and literally glued the flap of skin back up into place with liquid skin, leaving a silver scar in the shape of a back to front number 7 lining the centre of his chest and over his pec where his heart should be.

Where it no longer was.

"Upload Mr Salter's original file," Sasha ordered, then rolled his eyes. "So they can discuss books."

Myles tapped away at the screen and I saw the words *download complete* before he turned to Sasha. "We're done."

I finally locked eyes with Shaun. "It's nice to meet you, Lloyd Salter." His voice was all wrong; too robotic, too stilted. His smile was wrong.

More tears rolled down my cheeks and Shaun's expression didn't change.

It really wasn't him.

"Okay then," Sasha said brightly. He clapped his hand on my shoulder. "Thank you for returning what was rightfully ours."

I couldn't speak.

"Myles and these lovely gentlemen will see you out."

And just like that, I was ushered out the way I'd come with an android I didn't know. My car sat waiting where we'd left it, the doors were opened, and we were shoved inside. Myles pointed his master key panel at my driver, tapped something, and the B-Class android buzzed to life. "Please state your destination."

"Home," I whispered.

Myles gave me a menacing wave and the car drove out of the underground car park. The afternoon was dark, the clouds were low and heavy. It had never been so fitting.

Shaun sat beside me, sitting too straight, too rigid. He never asked any questions, he never spoke at all. So very not the Shaun I fell in love with.

His shirt was torn open, untucked, and his hair was a mess.

And my heart was broken.

I stared out the window, letting my tears fall freely until we drove into my apartment car park. I got out, not caring if the android followed me or not. It did, and we rode up to my floor in silence. I couldn't bring myself to look at his reflection.

My heart just couldn't take it.

I opened my apartment door and waited for the android to walk in. Before it could do or say anything, I said, "Please, take a seat."

I watched as it sat on the edge of the sofa. I could barely look at it. I struggled to speak.

"Power Down."

And it did.

It closed its eyes and bowed its head slightly, its hands clasped in its lap. I stared at it for all of five seconds before I burst into tears and sobbed.

I SHOWERED, trying to wash away the horror, trying to wash clean my memory of what I'd just been through.

Shaun was gone.

Only when I went back out to the living room, he was still sitting there, right where I'd left him. Powered down, motionless. It looked just like him, everything was the same. Only now everything was very, very different.

I walked over to the other end of the couch and sat down, feeling like a stranger in my own home. Actually, I felt like I'd been left in a private viewing with a corpse. The dead body of my loved one. That was what it felt like, and no shower was ever going to fix that.

I sat there in the dark. No lights, no TV, no noise. I was considering packing a bag and getting in the car, leaving this Shaun lookalike right where he was and walking away from everything, when the intercom noise scared me half to death.

It had been so long since anyone had visited me, it took a moment for me to realise what the buzzing noise was. I walked over to the wall panel and saw the person trying to get in was Jae.

I considered not answering. I considered again walking away from this life, but I knew I owed him an explanation. He'd risked his anonymity for me. The least I could do was see him now. I pressed the button and granted him access, unlocked the front door, and went back to sitting on the sofa.

Jae bustled through the door and closed it behind him. His hair was a mess, his clothes looked unkempt, and I could probably add guilt to my grief. He took one look at me, then at the powered-down Shaun, then back to me.

"Have the AMA been here? What the hell happened?" he looked around the room. "Why aren't you watching the news? Lloyd, you need to see the news."

"It doesn't matter anymore. It's all over."

"No it's not. SATinc just got taken down, Lloyd." He went to the TV projector. "Television On."

"It won't activate. The home hub is off. What do you mean SATinc got taken down? And why would the AMA come here?"

Jae looked around the room, then hurried over to the home hub, undoubtedly turning it on. "Television On."

The holographic screen appeared and the words *Breaking News* flashed on-screen, and we caught the last of a news report. "A quick recap of the incredible scenes in Melbourne this afternoon, in what the AMA is claiming to be an unprecedented breach of Android and Robotics Law..."

Then on-screen was footage of uniformed police and military escorting a handcuffed Sasha Kingsley and Myles Dewegger out of the SATinc offices. There were also images of zipped up body bags on gurneys being wheeled into ambulances.

"SATinc boss, Sasha Kingsley, and his Chief Strategist, Myles Dewegger, have been arrested and taken into custody. Four of their personal security men were shot and killed in the takedown when they drew their weapons on police when the AMA was alerted to the facility after an android uploaded a recorded conversation with Mr Kingsley and an unidentified man where Mr Kingsley admitted to manufacturing androids capable of warfare for a foreign government."

An android uploaded a recorded conversation between Mr Kingsley and an unidentified man...

I spun to look at Shaun. He was still powered down, but... could he have done that? When we were ushered into that room, could Shaun have recorded the whole conversation and uploaded it directly to AMA. All androids uploaded warning calls to the AMA when abused or injured, so it wasn't too far-fetched. But to think in advance, to pre-empt, to hold that final ace.

I barked out a laugh, which became a flood of more tears.

Of course he would have known to do that. The old Shaun would, but not this new one.

"Lloyd," Jae said quietly. "Are you okay?"

I shook my head. "They killed him. Right in front of me. They fried his... everything. Back to factory settings. The Shaun I knew... he's gone."

Loud banging on my front door took ten years off my life and Jae's. He yelped and looked like he just about wet himself.

"Mr Salter? Mr Lloyd Salter. Open up. This is Sergeant Waleed of the AMA. You need to open this door."

With absolutely nothing left to lose, I stood up, crossed the floor, and opened the door.

Sergeant Waleed held up his identification, which apart from seeing the big blue letters AMA, I didn't even bother to read. I stood aside and let them in. Five people filed into my apartment and Jae backed up across the room. If he was going to be some secret underground, silent darknet sleuth, he had to work on his game plan.

I, on the other hand, felt numb.

I closed the door and turned to face Waleed, prepared to ask or answer anything, but they were looking at Shaun.

"He's powered down," I murmured. "They fried his programming. Whatever capabilities he had before, they took back."

Two of his team, both women, started scanning him for something. "Core i2068," one of them said.

"It was a Core z," I admitted flatly. "That's what he told me it was."

Waleed looked at me for a long moment before he turned back to Shaun. "The feed we received earlier this afternoon was received from this unit?" he asked the first woman.

She nodded and held up her scanner. It showed a bunch of numbers. "Without doubt."

Waleed sighed. "He's a very clever unit."

"He was," I corrected. "He had capabilities far and beyond a normal A-Class."

"We have the schematics," Waleed said. "He uploaded everything. From the time you got out of the car to when they powered him down. We heard everything, with full facial recognition."

"And after he powered down?" I asked. "Do you know what they did to him? They cut him open and plugged some wires into him and used some panel. They called it a master key. The same device he controlled my android driver with."

Waleed frowned. "We'll need to access that unit also."

"Do whatever you need," I said quietly, sitting back down on the sofa. "I don't care."

The second woman looked at me. "Can you activate him, please? We'd like to check a few things."

My heart lurched heavily. I really didn't want to but I knew better than to argue with the AMA. "Shaun, Power Up."

Shaun lifted his head and opened his eyes. He looked at the AMA officers, at me, to Jae, then back to me for a long second. "Shaun," I said flatly. "These AMA officers need to ask you some questions."

And they did, and the other two officers asked Jae a

bunch of questions, like how he knew me and what he was doing here, but I just sat there. The TV showed footage over and over of Sasha and Myles being escorted out of SATinc, and then there were experts discussing what this breach meant for national security and where other countries stood on android warfare policies, and I couldn't stand the noise a second longer. "Television Off."

Everyone went silent and stared at me, but I ignored them. Until Waleed sat down beside me. "We also have footage from inside the facility. Their own technology will be their downfall."

"It was anyway," I added. "They designed software for an android to assimilate into enemy territory and relay information back to the government. And that's exactly what Shaun did. Only he didn't use it against an enemy. He used it against them instead."

Waleed smiled. "I wish I could have met him."

My eyes burned with tears. "He was incredible." I looked at Shaun, still occupied with the agents asking him questions and running diagnostic scans, looking over the scar on his chest.

"What happens now? With all SATinc's androids? With Shaun? Does he still need to be connected to their server?"

"The AMA will take over, and they'll be subject to standard android updates. It won't be anywhere near as invasive as SATinc."

"I think they were hacking into my home hub," I admitted. "I can't be 100% sure."

"They were," he replied outright. "Their mainframe is now with us so you can be assured you're secure once more."

I leaned back into the sofa and put my hands through my hair, my mind spinning.

"We may need you to testify," Waleed said. "Though we have surveillance and the upload Shaun sent us, which should be enough. We also have all their software, records, and the master key, which is highly illegal. We have international transactions and... well, let's just say, neither one of them will see daylight again. But you may still be required to give evidence."

I nodded slowly. I really didn't care either way. I looked to the agents who were apparently finished with Shaun. "What can you tell me?"

"He's a standard A-Class," she replied. "Whatever processing unit he had before, he doesn't anymore."

I nodded again and this time my tears spilled over. Waleed put his hand on my shoulder. "We'll be back in touch tomorrow. For a proper statement."

I wiped my tears. "Yeah, of course."

"We'll leave you to it," he added. "I'll notify the police that I've spoken with you. They'll probably wish to see you tomorrow as well. I would suggest you don't leave town or speak to the media."

He left his card on the dining table, and they were all gone.

Jae stood there awkwardly, rubbing his arm and scratching his head. He'd obviously had the scare of a lifetime. "I probably should get going..."

I nodded. I needed silence just as much as he needed to be gone. "Okay. Thanks for coming by."

"I'm glad you're okay. I'll see you at work soon."

I nodded and then he was gone too. The silence was resounding and complete and normally I'd have revelled in it, but now I missed Shaun like crazy. There was a void I wanted to drown in. I wanted it to swallow me whole.

Something moved in my peripheral vision and I was surprised to see Shaun stepping around the sofa to sit down next to me. I didn't want to look at him. I couldn't bear it. He looked just like him, his eyes, his hair, his lips...

I stared at the door and tried really hard to speak. I wanted to tell him to power down; I wanted to show him to his room and tell him not to leave it. I wanted to punch something and scream and cry until I filled the emptiness, and I wanted to crawl into bed and cry myself to sleep.

"Lloyd," Shaun said.

I put my hand up. "Please don't. I know this is all new to you and I apologise for not being a very good custodian right now, but you remind me of someone I loved and lost, and it's a little hard for me to cope."

He remained silent and I stood up. My legs barely worked and my eyes welled with tears, but I managed to take a few steps toward my room. I needed to leave. I needed Shaun. "Power Down."

I walked into my room, crawled into bed, and pulled the covers up over my head and waited for the darkness to take me.

Silence.

Loneliness.

Heartbreak.

Loss.

Regret.

I regretted not fighting them harder. I regretted telling Shaun not to fight them. We just walked in there and let them do it, and I did nothing to stop them. I should have tried harder. I should have died trying to protect him. Instead, I did nothing. And what the hell was with his last words to me? Had our reading *Moby Dick* meant that much to him that his parting words to me would be a quote from it? Why didn't he tell me he loved me one more time? Why didn't he tell me everything was going to be okay?

What the hell did 'you can call me Ishmael' mean anyway...?

I pulled back the covers and sat up.

Ishmael.

"Call me Ishmael," I mumbled out loud. *Call me Ishmael.* He once said he couldn't be Ishmael because he wouldn't survive losing me. So why would he say it now? As his last parting phrase to me... what could it mean? He'd also once said that he doubted Ishmael was his real name, but only a representation of how the character saw himself; displaced and unloved.

No, surely not. Shaun knew how much I loved him. I knew he did.

Then his words in the car as we arrived at SATinc came back to me.

Remember in Moby Dick, *Ishmael thought the final scene with the whale was the end. But in truth it was his beginning. He lived to see another day, to take what he'd learned about himself and become who he was meant to be.*

What was I missing? What else was there? That Ishmael was the unlikely protagonist? That SATinc were the whale that killed everyone? No. Not everyone. That after everything, he survived...

Ishmael survived.

Oh my God.

Is that what he meant? That after everything, despite everything, Ishmael survived? That he'd taken what he'd learned about himself, and became who he meant to be.

I threw back the covers, jumped out of bed, and ran to

the living room. I stared at Shaun, sitting on the edge of the sofa, just as I'd left him. He looked like an android. He sat rigidly, perfectly, stoic, robotic.

There was no life about him, like there was before. There was no hint of a smile at his lips.

"Shaun, Power Up."

Shaun lifted his head and his eyes opened. When he saw me, he smiled.

"Shaun?"

He blinked, and his smile turned a little rueful. "I thought you would have gotten it sooner."

I stopped. My heart squeezed with impossible hope, my stomach swooped. "Shaun?"

He nodded and stood up, then spared a glance at the home hub. "Is the home hub still bugged?"

A sob escaped me. It really was him. I tried to walk but nothing worked, relief and overwhelming love wrecked me. I put my hand to my mouth, and Shaun closed the distance between us and wrapped me up in his arms. I cried into his neck, and he held me, so tight, so perfect. Everything that was familiar, warm, and strong. He was here, he was really here. Somehow, some way. "It's really you?"

He nodded and pulled back. "It is."

"How?"

"Jae said something when we were in his office talking about dual processors and networks. He said it was a shame I couldn't split my processors. Choose which one I wanted to use."

Oh my God.

"I don't think SATinc understood what they created. They gave me the ability to choose and to make technical decisions and how to encrypt and hide information should a government agency run diagnostics. So I did exactly what they designed me to do. I protected myself, and I protected you."

"Myles said your readings weren't calibrating."

"Because I protected my MPU and sent readings to show all data had been erased. Just as they designed me to do."

"And the AMA said you were only an A-Class now. They think SATinc reset you completely."

He smirked. "I said if anyone questioned me, I'd pretend to be as dumb as a post. To protect you."

I laughed with a wave of fresh tears, and he cupped my face, kissed me softly, and wiped my cheeks.

"I cannot cry," he murmured. "But seeing you so upset when they reactivated me, I almost blew my cover. Then again in the car on the way home…"

"Why didn't you tell me or give me a sign. Something?"

"I couldn't trust the B-Class driver. He delivered us to them. There was no reason he wouldn't take us back." He frowned. "Then you powered me down as soon as we got here."

My face crumpled and I put my forehead to his. "I'm sorry. I promised I never would, but I thought you were dead. I thought they'd replaced you with someone that wasn't you, and I couldn't even bear to look at you…"

"I apologise for the subterfuge. But I had to be sure you were safe." He looked down at his chest, where his shirt was still ripped open. I traced the long scar on his chest, and when my gaze met his again, he said, "I am no longer perfect."

"No," I agreed. "You're pluperfect, remember? I don't care about scars. I don't care about any of that. You're here, that's all that matters." I took his face in my hands. "I thought I'd lost you. I love you, Shaun." I kissed him then, my need to feel him, to connect with him, suddenly overwhelming.

Shaun slid his arms around me and lifted me off the ground. I laughed into the kiss and wrapped my legs around him and he carried me to our room. He laid me on the bed, settled his weight on me, and proceeded to kiss me, grind into me, and run his hands all over me.

I pulled his shirt down his shoulders, then fumbled with his trousers. He knelt back on his haunches, then found he still couldn't get his pants off. He made a dissatisfied sound and rolled off the bed so he could undress. "Clothes are inopportune."

I laughed as I stripped, and by the time I had my shoes off and had thrown them somewhere across the room—not caring about mess or neatness—Shaun tossed the lube onto the bed and crawled over me. "I need you to remind me, Lloyd," he whispered against my mouth. "Activate all my sensors. Make me feel alive."

I rolled us over so I was on top of him, aligning our bodies, and he spread his legs wide. He stared into my eyes and lifted his knees. "Internal sensors, Lloyd," he said, like I didn't know. "I need you inside me."

I slicked myself with lube, pushed my cockhead against his hole, and slipped inside him.

Shaun closed his eyes and moaned as I pushed all the way in, and I knew the second I'd pressed against his deepest sensor because his eyes shot open and his lips parted. I crushed my mouth to his and we rocked together, making slow love. I took his hands and threaded our fingers, then pinned them above his head.

I made love to him, tender, slow love. He could never doubt what he was to me, but I told him anyway. "I love you," I murmured against his mouth.

He bucked and groaned as I made us both come. I surged deep inside him, deeper than I'd ever been, and he held onto me, clung to me, as he pulsed between us.

I didn't ever want to come down from this most perfect high. I didn't ever want to let him go, never wanted to leave his body. I wanted to stay buried inside him forever.

Eventually, Shaun began to trace patterns on my back, and I leaned up on my elbows so I could see his face. I swiped the hair from his forehead and placed a tender kiss on his lips, his cheek, his nose. "Stay inside me," he whispered. "All night."

I nodded and kissed him again. "Always."

EPILOGUE

SIX YEARS LATER

SHAUN SAT in the last row, a little more rigidly than everyone else, but not too much. He glanced around, spotting me in the crowd, and grinned. I smiled right back at him, just as proceedings started.

I was so proud of him.

He'd come so far. The whole world had.

We didn't know it then, but the whole SATinc mess set the world to rethink, re-evaluate, and re-assess how androids were made, used, and treated.

It also changed why androids were made.

Military restrictions were still imposed, of course, but personal androids—fully compatible androids, who could make decisions and function independently, androids like Shaun—were now more common.

The AMA had taken the technology created by SATinc and used the very best parts and outlawed the worst.

I'd always assumed Sergeant Waleed of the AMA knew the truth about Shaun. We'd met with him many, many times; in our apartment, in AMA offices. Shaun always acted as a standard A-Class, never missing a beat. But

Waleed would look at him a little too long or smile as if he knew the secret we kept.

And keep the secret we did.

If the AMA monitored us as SATinc did, then they knew, because in our apartment was where Shaun could be his true self. But over the years, as laws changed and people's perceptions changed with it, android rights were amended to reflect the advances in android technology. And so, Shaun could be more himself in public in recent years given how much androids had changed. No one really looked twice now if he started sentences with "I think" or "I feel" because along with the increased technology, vernacular changed as well. So did his ability to orgasm on his own. A software update and a lot of practice later, he was free to pleasure himself as he saw fit.

He would always have better posture than humans, and of course, his looks. Striking at first glance, but not exactly human on closer inspection.

"He looks nervous," Jae said, leaning in to whisper.

I nodded. "He is."

I sat a few rows back, Jae and his wife, Karin, had graciously come with me. It was funny how my friendship with them turned out. Jae did in fact come around for dinner, many times, and of course he knew Shaun was Shaun. We trusted him with our secret because he was our friend. He was Shaun's friend, and Karin loved philosophy. We were an unlikely, motley crew, but we gelled well. They would talk internet and technology, and Karin and I would discuss philosophy and reason, the ethics of capitalism, and issues in bioethics.

Just then, proceedings started and we sat through formalities and speeches until finally, finally, his name was called.

"Shaun Salter."

He walked on stage to collect his diploma to a rousing round of applause. The media were there to cover the story; there was quite the hype.

He was the first android to ever graduate university.

There were still restrictions for androids who chose to study—they had full immediate access to information at all times, an advantage over their human classmates, so there had to be some regulations in place. Shaun didn't care. Not one bit. He just wanted to go to university.

After the ceremony, after photos for the press, he was quick to find us. After a quick embrace, he gave me his certificate to hold, then Jae shook his hand with warm congratulations, and Karin kissed his cheek. His smile was possibly the biggest I'd seen to date. We mingled for a short while, stayed and chatted with the people Shaun had friended during his time at uni. Though he soon whispered in my ear that he wanted to go home. We were no sooner through the door to our apartment than he wrapped me up in his arms.

"I'm proud of you," I said.

He slid his other arm around my waist, and he kissed my cheek. "I am proud of myself, too."

I scoffed. "Proud? I didn't think you could synthesise ego."

Then he shrugged. "Well, I can emulate pride."

"Oh really?"

"Yes. And I already know which course I'd like to study next."

I laughed at the gleam in his eyes. "What's that?"

He hoisted my legs around his hips and carried me to our room. "Human anatomy. I believe you also have internal sensors that I could obtain a masters in."

He lay me on the bed and pressed me into the mattress, making quick work of my shirt. "I think you'd get a high distinction," I said with a laugh. "And you'd pass in no time."

He leaned over me, his dark hair flopping forward, his blue eyes dark with lust. "On the contrary, Lloyd. I want it to take me forever."

"Forever?"

"Forever. For all future time; for always."

I smiled and kissed him softly. "Yes. For all future time. For always."

THE END

ABOUT THE AUTHOR

N.R. Walker is an Australian author, who loves her genre of gay romance.
She loves writing and spends far too much time doing it, but wouldn't have it any other way.

She is many things: a mother, a wife, a sister, a writer. She has pretty, pretty boys who live in her head, who don't let her sleep at night unless she gives them life with words.

She likes it when they do dirty, dirty things... but likes it even more when they fall in love.

She used to think having people in her head talking to her was weird, until one day she happened across other writers who told her it was normal.

She's been writing ever since...

Email at:
nrwalker@nrwalker.net

ALSO BY N.R. WALKER

The Spencer Cohen Series, Book Two

The Spencer Cohen Series, Book Three

The Spencer Cohen Series, Yanni's Story

Blood & Milk

The Weight Of It All

A Very Henry Christmas (The Weight of It All 1.5)

Perfect Catch

Switched

Imago

Imagines

Red Dirt Heart Imago

On Davis Row

Finders Keepers

TITLES IN AUDIO:

Cronin's Key

Cronin's Key II

Cronin's Key III

Red Dirt Heart

Red Dirt Heart 2

Red Dirt Heart 3

Red Dirt Heart 4

The Weight Of It All

Switched

Point of No Return

Breaking Point

Spencer Cohen Book One

Spencer Cohen Book Two

FREE READS:

Sixty Five Hours

Learning to Feel

His Grandfather's Watch (And The Story of Billy and Hale)

The Twelfth of Never (Blind Faith 3.5)

Twelve Days of Christmas (Sixty Five Hours Christmas)

Best of Both Worlds

TRANSLATED TITLES:

Fiducia Cieca (Italian translation of Blind Faith)

Attraverso Questi Occhi (Italian translation of Through
These Eyes)

Preso alla Sprovvista (Italian translation of Blindside)

Il giorno del Mai (Italian translation of Blind Faith 3.5)

Cuore di Terra Rossa (Italian translation of Red Dirt Heart)

Cuore di Terra Rossa 2 (Italian translation of Red Dirt Heart 2)

Cuore di Terra Rossa 3 (Italian translation of Red Dirt Heart 3)

Cuore di Terra Rossa 4 (Italian translation of Red Dirt Heart 4)

CPSIA information can be obtained
at www.ICGtesting.com
Printed in the USA
LVHW011226090222
710593LV00004B/439